Other Novels by Clare Jayne

CONTENTS

Lady Tinbough's Dilemma (Campbell & MacPherson 1)

First Novel of the Historical Mystery Series

Clare Jayne

1. STUDYING CRIME

Edinburgh Court of Justiciary - 27 August 1788

"HOW IRONIC – the thief is the best-dressed man in the courtroom!"

The words were spoken in a lively, amused tone and Ishbel paused in her own examination of the plaintiff, William Brodie, and glanced behind her. The young man who had spoken was little older than her own eighteen years and the splendour of his own outfit made a lie of his words. Indeed, she could see beyond him the groups of upper-class ladies in wide panelled dresses and gentlemen in bright colours and with powdered hair, dressed as if they were attending a ball. The slender man behind her caught her gaze and smiled disarmingly, the eyes that met hers a clear grass-green.

She hastily looked away, a slight heat rising to her cheeks, then an official announced the judges and everyone got to their feet. The five men were striking in their scarlet robes – it seemed as if everyone wanted the title of best-dressed person here. Everyone except her. Ishbel's own gown was an old plain one – she had had the foolish idea that she would be the only member of Edinburgh society to attend the trial, not that she would have dressed any better had she suspected the truth. She had no interest in clothes and just as little in finding a husband, so she did her best to ignore society and, on the occasions Harriette dragged her to some so-called entertainment, society was equally happy to ignore her.

The judges took their seats and, with much scraping of wooden chairs over floor, everyone else in the courtroom followed suit, the earlier chatter fading away as the trial began.

"William Brodie," one of the court officials intoned loudly, "sometime wright and cabinetmaker in Edinburgh, and George Smith, sometime grocer there, both prisoners in the Tolbooth of Edinburgh, you are indicted and accused..."

Ishbel reached into her reticule and removed a quill, new bottle of ink and several sheets of parchment. Lucy, her lady's maid, took the ink from her, un-stoppered it and held it out. Lucy gave her a quick grateful smile then began her notes of the trial. She looked again at the prisoner and took in, for the first time, the fact that there were in fact two prisoners. Brodie was being tried alongside one of his accomplices in the attempted robbery of the General Excise Office. The other man, Smith, looked haggard and shabby next to the elegance of Brodie in his dark coat, bright waistcoat, silk breeches and powdered, dressed hair. Smith's expression was miserable while Brodie gazed upon the man reading the charges with the calm interest of one in no way ruffled by any of these proceedings.

Ishbel scribbled down her observations about the prisoners and noted the charges against them. She glanced up to see the prisoners get to their feet, so the head judge, Lord Braxfield, could address them. When he asked if they were guilty of the crimes of which they were accused a stillness fell over the room as everyone strained to hear their responses.

"My lord, I am not guilty," Brodie said and, as Smith echoed the words, there were some gasps from the members of the public and someone called out, "Yes, you are!"

Braxfield banged his gavel sharply on the bench, the loud noise making Ishbel spill ink over her notes. She hastily found a handkerchief and, ignoring Lucy's slight tut at ruining the linen, she used it to soak up the excess ink. Lucy held out a hand, palm up, to take the stained cloth, expression fondly exasperated, and Ishbel grimaced and passed over the handkerchief.

By this time Lord Braxfield was swearing in the fifteen members of the jury who would decide the fate of Brodie and Smith. Braxfield's Scottish accent was broad and his expression fierce - he was said to have been friends with Brodie's father and she wondered how that affected him now. Did that make him more inclined to treat the son with severity or lenience? She scribbled down this question

2

then caught a movement out of the corner of her eye and glanced round to see the smart gentleman behind her leaning forward to see what she was writing.

She ignored him with difficulty, self-conscious as she returned to her notes.

Witness after witness was called to give evidence against William Brodie – Deacon Brodie as he was more commonly known due to his former position as a Deacon of Wrights and cabinetmaker, someone who – ironically – had been admitted to people's houses to put in stronger locks and protect them from burglars just like him. He looked eminently respectable save for the scar on his face and she wondered how he had come by the mark. The prosecution were painting him as a wretch who feigned respectability but spent his nights either gambling or, with a black mask over his face, robbing wealthy people who had trusted him with their house keys.

When another witness was proposed, a strong, melodic voice said, "My lords, I object!"

Ishbel looked up and saw a slender back of Mr Erskine, Brodie's solicitor, who had risen to his feet and spoken. She recognised him from various balls and formal dinners that he had attended with his brothers, the Earl of Buchan and Baron Erskine. Mr Erskine's objection was overruled and Ishbel caught a look of anger on the faces of Brodie and Smith as they turned their heads to watch a witness walk forward and take the stand. It was the first strong emotion Brodie had shown all day so she moved her gaze with interest to the rough-looking man who was giving his oath to speak the truth.

"That is the one who betrayed Brodie and had them all arrested." The quiet, well-spoken words came once again from the gentleman behind her but she did not turn to see whom he addressed.

Another male voice replied: "Who is he?"

"An accomplice in the robberies."

They fell silent as the man began to give his evidence, the information detailed and damning. Ishbel looked to see how Brodie and Smith were reacting and saw that Brodie had regained his composure, his bearing almost regal as he looked at the witness. She could not see Smith's expression, her view of him only revealing the back of a plain coat and greasy-looking hair. He had been incarcerated for some months while Brodie had been on the run –

fleeing to Amsterdam – and prison life had clearly not been easy for Smith.

Another accomplice of Brodie's was called to give evidence against him and Erskine's objection was once more overruled.

"Politics," commented the gentleman behind Ishbel. "The Tories will never let the Whigs win here."

Ishbel looked with a fresh gaze upon the people in front of her, realising for the first time that, from the political standing of those she recognised, the judges and those prosecuting the prisoners were indeed Tories while those defending the prisoners were members of the more liberal Whig party. That explained some of the tensions she had not before understood and anger rose in her at the thought that two men, whose lives were at stake, might in part be victims of political machinations that should have no place in a trial.

It was late evening before the case for the prosecution was concluded and Ishbel, not knowing how trials were conducted, expected it to end for the day and be resumed tomorrow. Instead Mr Erskine stood up and began his defence case for Brodie.

"It's getting late, Miss," Lucy whispered to her.

Ishbel agreed and glanced round, noting that the courtroom was less full than it had been earlier, a dozen or so people never having returned after the earlier adjournment for dinner. Still, she could not go now and miss important details. It would surely not go on for too much longer.

"Take the sedan chair back to the house," she whispered to Lucy, "then send it back to wait for me."

"Certainly not, Miss. If you are staying then so am I."

Ishbel opened her mouth to argue further then took in Lucy's pursed mouth and slight frown and gave in, glad she would not be on her own later, although it would hardly have been the first time she had made her way to her cousin's home alone late at night. She took her maid's free hand – the one not holding the ink bottle – and squeezed it.

Mr Erskine called a striking, dark-haired woman by the name of Jean Watt to the stand and she gave evidence – in a convincing tone – that Mr Brodie had been with her and their children for the entire night when the Excise Office robbery had taken place. Their children? Mr Brodie was unmarried.

Gasps and muttered comments went around the courtroom as the listeners absorbed this shocking information then Ishbel heard a woman's voice – high-pitched and distressed. People's heads turned and Ishbel tried to catch sight of who was speaking, seeing a middle-aged woman at the same time as the loud knocking of Lord Braxfield's gavel sounded.

"Who is that?" a man behind her asked. Not her gen – not the gentleman who had smiled at her earlier, she corrected herself, but the one he had presumably been addressing his comments to.

"I have no idea but the poor woman looks distressed." That was his voice – aristocratic but gentle – and the concern in his tone warmed her to him.

She glanced back at the middle-aged woman who had a hand over her mouth as if to choke back a further outcry. A younger woman – her daughter perhaps given their similarity of features – put an arm round her and spoke in what looked like an urgent manner.

After a minute they settled down and Ishbel focused on the witnesses – Jean Watt, then her young son and maid – who all swore Mr Brodie had been with them when the robbery was occurring. She lost track of time as she wrote down her impressions of what was said and by whom.

She was smothering a yawn when a young man stood up and began to speak. From his words on his client's behalf, he was clearly one of the people defending George Smith, the second prisoner, but she had not caught his name.

The lawyer referred to the testimonies of the two accomplices of Brodie and Smith, saying to the jury in a loud, lively manner that caught everyone's attention, "Gentlemen, you have heard a variety of objections stated to the admissibility of their evidence – all of which have been overruled by the court. But, notwithstanding the judgements of their Lordships, I must adhere to these objections and maintain that they ought not to have been admitted as witnesses. I think a great deal of most improper evidence has been received in this case for the Crown."

By the time he had finished this indictment everyone in the courtroom was wide awake and Ishbel peered round the tall gentleman in front of her, trying to see the reactions of the five judges. She had little time to wait, several of the scarlet-robed men objecting to the negative assessment of their handling of the trial.

The defence lawyer was only just beginning. He called one of the accomplices who had given evidence against Smith and Brodie a villain, saying that, having been convicted of a crime in England, "how dare he come here to be received as a witness in this case?"

The main prosecution lawyer glared at his colleague and said, "He has, as I have shown you, received His Majesty's free pardon."

"Yes, I see, but, gentlemen of the jury, I ask you on your oaths, can His Majesty make a tainted scoundrel an honest man?"

Ishbel was startled into laughter at this and a burst of appreciative applause for the lawyer sounded from around her. She wished she knew his name. He then got into a heated argument with Lord Braxfield about whether or not the jury should listen to the judges' opinions of the case. When Lord Braxfield, whose accent grew broader the angrier he got, attempted to move the case forward and call upon Brodie's defence lawyer, Smith's lawyer actually shook his fist in the air, exclaiming, "Hang my client if you dare, my lord, without hearing me in his defence!"

Ishbel breathed in sharply at this and, as another burst of applause sounded from the thoroughly entertained watchers, she looked to see how the judges would respond. Lord Braxfield had a murderous look in his eyes but allowed himself to be talked into adjourning the case so the judges could decide how to proceed.

Everyone got to their feet as the judges stood and, as one, marched out of the courtroom.

"Well, you were quite right, MacPherson," one of the men behind her said, difficult to hear in the roar of noise from everyone talking at once. "This was far more entertaining than an appointment with my tailor and an evening at the tavern."

She had a name for the green-eyed gentleman now: Mr MacPherson. He said, "Good lord, it is nearly three in the morning."

At these words Ishbel could not help giving a yawn. She hoped Harriette and Lord Huntly would not be concerned at her absence. No, she remembered. They had been due to attend a ball at the Assembly Rooms tonight and would, no doubt, not yet be home themselves.

Beside her, Lucy rubbed her eyes and Ishbel felt a stab of guilt at having kept up like this. Lucy worked long enough hours and had a sufficiently difficult life – most of the money she made going to help her parents and siblings – that she should not have had to be here on Ishbel's whim.

"Tomorrow – once we get home today, that is – you must take the full day and night off to catch up on your sleep," she said.

"That's not necessary, Miss."

"Yes, it is," Ishbel insisted.

Lucy took in her mistress's resolute expression and said, "Thanks then, that'll be nice. Just as long as you get some rest too and don't instantly run off to the university."

Ishbel – who had been intending to do exactly that – made a non-committal sound. She glanced down and, with horror, realised that tiredness had made her forget all about her writing. She had not recorded anything for probably more than an hour. She hastily lifted her quill and, ignoring the sigh beside her, recommenced scribbling. It made no difference that no one but her would ever be likely to read her account – it needed to be accurate and complete.

She had barely got started when the judges returned, looking calmer than when they had left. The case moved forward with the brash lawyer finishing his impassioned defence of George Smith and Mr Erskine standing up to give a brief but well-spoken conclusion to his own defence of William Brodie. Lord Buxfield then gave the view of the judges, which was that both prisoners were guilty, and the case was adjourned for the jury to make their own decision.

"Oh, no," Lucy complained as the judges left the courtroom, "I thought it was over. What should we do now?"

Ishbel tried to shake the fog of exhaustion and make her mind function with any degree of clarity. "We will go home," she said, "and I will send one of the footmen to wait and send for me to hear the verdict. Your duties are now entirely over."

"Yes, Miss." Lucy smiled in her usual amiable way and they got wearily to their feet and headed outside, with the rest of the crowd, to find Lord Huntly's sedan. It was only when they were seated in it on the way back to her cousin's grand house that Ishbel remembered the green-eyed gentleman – Mr MacPherson – who had sat behind her. She would no doubt never see him again and found herself regretting that fact.

2. THE VERDICT

"I WILL let you tell me the verdict," Chiverton said to Ewan MacPherson as they left the courthouse, emerging from the gloom into hot August sunshine nearly a full day and night after they had entered the building. "I desire only my bed." He yawned widely to prove the fact.

Ewan was only half listening as he watched the red-haired woman vanish out of sight in the crowd. Why would a well-dressed lady have been writing notes about the case and why, when everyone else in the audience had simply wanted to be entertained, had she taken the proceedings so seriously?

"Do you see an acquaintance?" Chiverton asked, following his gaze with sleepy curiosity.

Ewan turned and smiled at his old friend. "I was just lost in thought."

"Asleep on your feet, more like." Chiverton dusted off his purple coat, always liking to look his best, which set the standard high for everyone around him. He then gestured to Ewan's sleeve and made a tutting sound. "Your valet will never forgive you."

Ewan looked down and saw a smudge of black on the arm of his greatcoat. He brushed at it to no effect. "Damn!"

"If either of us is awake tonight, I might see you at the Cape Club."

"Perhaps." Ewan was rather bored of the club with its mix of drunken men all telling increasingly unlikely tales of their sexual escapades, perhaps in part because he had no tales of his own to tell, his life the picture of uneventful respectability.

They parted and Ewan strode through streets that were surprisingly busy and noisy at such an inhuman hour, wagons of food and goods being unloaded into shops, stalls being set up, working class Scottish voices calling out to each other and the odour of food and horse manure in the air. His stomach reminded him that he had not eaten in around twelve hours so he paused to buy a meat pie before continuing, relaxing when he reached the silent, unmoving peace of the residential street where his three-storey Old Town house stood.

He raised his hand to open the door but MacCuaig, his butler, reached it first and Ewan smiled and stepped into the large hallway, pausing to hand over his tricorne hat.

"I trust you had a good night," MacCuaig asked, heavily lined face blank but the coolness of his tone penetrating Ewan's sleepy brain.

"I should have sent word," he said apologetically. "I had no idea the trial would go on until such an hour and the verdict is not yet in. I will leave again within the hour but if Mrs Middleton could put together some form of breakfast in the meantime I would be grateful."

"We are all here to serve you, sir," MacCuaig said, unthawed. "At whatever hour."

Ewan headed to his bed chamber to wash and change and found his valet, Rabbie, waiting.

"I did not intend to wake the household," Ewan said as the young man walked forward to help him change.

Rabbie gave him an amused look, their similarity of ages and his own nature making Ewan view his valet more as a friend than a servant. "It was no trouble. The staff are mostly awake every day at sunrise."

"Good lord, really?"

Ewan removed his blue coat and handed it to Rabbie, who caught sight of the smudge on its sleeve, all brightness fading into an expression of horror. He raised his eyes to give Ewan a wounded look. "I trust the court case was worth such a price."

"It is not yet over. I will return soon to hear the verdict," Ewan ventured.

"Yes, sir." Rabbie's normally friendly tone was neutral, registering his annoyance as clearly as MacCuaig's tone had.

"After today I doubt I shall ever attend another trial," Ewan said in appeasement. "Nothing else could match up to the grandness and notoriety of Brodie's case."

Rabbie accepted the crumpled cravat Ewan had unwound from his neck and, in a brighter manner, asked, "I'm sure your decision is for the best, sir. You have too much going on in your life with all the balls and card games and such-like to fit in many days like the last one."

Ewan could not have said why he felt a twinge of regret upon hearing these words since his life did hold more than enough amusements to fill his time. He thought, not for the first time, that he must find a wife - marriage and children would bring his life more meaning.

Rabbie poured water from jug into basin and Ewan washed his face and underarms, the cold water refreshing him and bringing his sluggish senses back to life. A few minutes later, clad in a new outfit of turquoise breeches with matching jacket and turquoise-and-white striped waistcoat, he walked to the dining room and helped himself to breakfast. Mrs Middleton, at least, must not be annoyed with him since she had provided the fresh strawberries he loved along with cooked food and ale.

Not wanting to miss the end of Brodie's trial, Ewan did not linger at home. He refused the suggestion of a sedan chair – causing MacCuaig, who had served his more conservative father for decades, to look at him as if Ewan were a troublesome child – and swiftly walked back to the large courthouse on Parliament Square. Taking a sedan chair or curricle might better befit Ewan's status as one of the landed upper-classes but he enjoyed the chance to get some decent exercise and the opportunity to see more of Edinburgh's population.

St Giles' Church bells struck eight o'clock as he joined the throng of people outside the court. He quickly struck up a conversation with several merchants as they all waited for the jury to return.

"I still find it difficult to believe that someone as well respected and wealthy as Mr Brodie could have behaved in such an appalling manner," the oldest member of the group said. He was a smart but plainly dressed man with more grey than brown in his tied back hair. "What would possibly make him don mask and go off to rob people, many of whom had previously employed him?"

"I expect it cost a bit to house his mistress and that child," a younger man said with a smirk.

"Two mistresses, Black," the third man – a sandy haired fellow dressed in orange clothes – corrected him, "and any number of children."

"Two mistresses?" Ewan asked, startled.

"Aye. Did you see the commotion in court when the first mistress gave evidence?"

"A woman got upset," Ewan remembered, frowning.

"She was the other one. Hadn't known a thing about Potts, the first mistress, until today."

"Disgraceful," the older man said.

"True," the sandy haired man agreed, "but Brodie obviously wrung every bit of pleasure he could from his wild life. You cannae help admiring him for that."

"I can," the older man said shortly. "He'll deservedly hang for this."

"Do you not think transportation more likely?" Ewan suggested. "After all, he never killed or harmed anyone."

"Hanging," the older man insisted.

"I think they'll just chop a hand off," Black said and Ewan winced inwardly at the thought and wondered what was going through Brodie's mind as he sat in prison now.

A few more hours passed by and Ewan was thinking of luncheon when a court officer told them the jury were back with a verdict. They all hurried inside and took seats then, as they waited for the judges, Ewan remembered the lovely woman who had been there earlier. He looked round the large room and sea of faces then spotted her distinctive red hair as she hurried in and took a place just a couple of rows behind him. He was finally able to see more than a glimpse of her face and was charmed by the view of red curls and wide-brimmed hat framing a delicate oval face with dark eyes and small full lips. She noticed his glance and he saw recognition enter her eyes. He smiled and stood to make a quick bow to her and her cheeks dimpled as her mouth quirked upwards.

The judges were announced and, mood buoyed by that smile, he turned to face the front of the courtroom as they walked in and took their places. A sealed piece of parchment was carried from the jury to the judges and the sentences were pronounced: guilty.

The room fell still and silent as Lord Braxfield said, "The

prisoners William Brodie and George Smith to be carried from the bar to the Tolbooth of Edinburgh, therein to be detained till Wednesday, the first day of October next, and upon that day to be taken forth of the said Tolbooth to the place fixed upon by the magistrates of Edinburgh as a common place of execution, and then and there, betwixt the hours of two and four o'clock afternoon to be hanged by the necks, by the hands of the Common Executioner, upon a gibbet, until they be dead."

The unnatural silence persisted and Ewan looked over at the two prisoners. Smith looked as one would expect: white-faced and dull-eyed. Brodie brought a hand up to his chest, a theatrical gesture, and, as all eyes fell on him, took a step forward and opened his mouth to speak.

Ewan held his breath and waited for his final words but the lawyer put a hand on the prisoner's arm, muttering in his ear, and Brodie closed his mouth, and let himself be led away by members of the town guard, their red military coats making Ewan think uneasily of blood and the spectre of death that hung over everyone.

The judges had left and the audience in the courtroom were talking or leaving by the time Ewan got to his feet. He turned to the seat where the red-haired lady had been, hoping to find out her name and exchange a few words, but, to his disappointment, she had already left.

As he walked away from his seat he noticed something white on the floor beneath the chair the lovely stranger had sat in. He bent down and picked it up: it was a lady's handkerchief with an elaborately embroidered letter 'I' on it.

"I need to find a young lady and hoped you might be able to help me," Ewan Campbell said to his aunt, Lady Morrelly. She knew every titled and land-owning family in Edinburgh so, having been unable to get the woman out of his mind all day, he had confidence that his aunt would be able to tell him who she was.

Sitting in her parlour with an abandoned piece of embroidery on the chair arm and a cup of tea and large slice of cake on the coffee table beside her, his aunt's eyes lit up at these words, clearly reading more into his interest than he had intended. "Indeed. What is her name?"

"I do not know," he admitted as a large cat with long white fur jumped onto the chair beside him then stepped onto his lap, moved in a circle then sunk down on him. He stroked the silky fur until the air was filled with the soft sound of purring and, after a night without sleep, he struggled against its soporific effect.

"Which family is she related to?"

"I have no idea. She dropped this and I wish to return it to her." He held out the lady's handkerchief, having to lean forward to pass it to his aunt and the cat made an annoyed sound and dug her claws into his legs, sending pricking pains through them. He resumed his petting and her grip relaxed.

Lady Morrelly examined the handkerchief as she said, "My dear, it is pleasant to see you showing an interest in a young lady but perhaps now you see the wisdom in obtaining a proper introduction so that you at least know the name of your future wife."

Ewan started at this. He had liked the woman but they had not even spoken yet. He had not intended to fall on one knee when he saw her again, although he did hope for a chance to get to know her better.

"You are, of course, looking to marry in the immediate future." Lady Morrelly fixed him with a look of heartfelt hope.

"Certainly," he agreed amenably.

"Do you happen to recall anything of this lady's appearance?"

"She had red hair," he said with satisfaction.

"Eye colour?"

Ewan looked up at the painted ceiling and tried to visualise the woman he had seen. "They were dark so I would say either brown or black, although they might have seemed darker than they were in the dim light of the courtroom so it is possible they were blue or green." At his aunt's sigh, he added, "The handkerchief has the letter 'T' on it and she was clearly a lady, although her clothes were unremarkable."

"Do you mean that she looked untidy or dressed badly?"

"Neither," he said at once, feeling he was letting down the unknown woman with such remarks. Perhaps he should not have approached his aunt for help after all. He tried to put his comment in a more complimentary form: "I had the impression that she had more important matters on her mind than dress."

Lady Morrelly gasped. "Ewan, I know that you had a mother since she was my sister, but I cannot imagine what she taught you about women if she did not impress upon you the necessity of a lady knowing how to dress well. Where did you say you encountered this person?"

He had deliberately not said. He braced himself before he did so now: "At the trial of the thief, William Brodie."

She fell backwards in her chair as if about to swoon.

"She wore a brooch!" he remembered. "It was in the shape of a flower – the flower was purple." He looked at her eagerly and she sat up and responded with the same disgruntled expression her cat had aimed at him once when he refused to feed it fish heads.

"Yes, I am aware of that young lady: Miss Ishbel Campbell." Her tone made it clear that this knowledge was no good thing but then she unexpectedly smiled. "I believe you will find her at the home of her cousin, Lady Huntly."

Ewan froze, his endeavour suddenly taking a deadly turn. Lady Huntly was one of the most influential women in Edinburgh. She was always invited to the most exclusive dinner parties and balls and their success or failure rested on her opinion. When she cut someone, as she frequently did, they lost all standing in society. She was said to bring men, women and children to tears on a daily basis.

Lady Morrelly was still smiling sweetly as she said, "I look forward to hearing the outcome of this little adventure of yours, my dear."

3. HARRIETTE INTERFERES

THE BUTLER entered the parlour while Harriette was in the middle of berating Ishbel about propriety. Since she was somewhat in the wrong on this occasion, Ishbel stood silently in the face of Harriette's comments and admonishments. Sharing titian hair and brown eyes, the two women were said to have a similar appearance – one unfortunate lady, never seen in polite society again, had thought them mother and daughter – but Ishbel hoped she would never have so fierce an expression on her face.

"... Clearly you do not care about ruining your reputation, but I will not allow you to sully that of our family by turning up at all hours of the night for some ludicrous reason. As long as you live under this roof..." Harriette broke off as she noticed the butler. "What is it, Gallach?"

"A gentleman is here to see Miss Ishbel, my lady."

The butler stepped forward and held out a silver tray. Ishbel took the white card off it and Harriette looked over her shoulder to read it and demand, "Who is this Mr MacPherson?"

Ishbel was at a loss. She did not think he was a student at the university but that was her only guess. "I do not know."

"Then let us find out," Harriette said and strode out, heading for the drawing room, Ishbel hurrying after her, a bit irritated that Harriette was interfering although she knew she would not have been allowed to speak to a gentleman without a chaperone being present. Here, at least, Ishbel was forced to conform to the ridiculous proprieties of the upper-classes.

They entered the drawing room and Ishbel instantly recognised the slender gentleman with the soulful green eyes from the courthouse. He gave them a wide smile and a graceful bow. Harriette's curtsy was of course perfect while Ishbel felt herself wobble slightly as she straightened from her own.

"Are we acquainted with you, Mr MacPherson?" Harriette asked in her usual quelling manner.

"I met Mr MacPherson at the courthouse yesterday," Ishbel hastened to explain, although *met* was an exaggeration since they had never actually spoken.

"Indeed." Harriette looked far from reassured by this, her manner remaining forbidding.

"I apologise for the intrusion," Mr MacPherson said at once. "I came to return this." He held out the handkerchief Ishbel had lost — having ruined one handkerchief with ink recently, her maid Lucy would be pleased to have this one safely back. Ishbel too was glad as this would save her an inconvenient visit to the shops to buy more.

Ishbel took the cloth from him. "Thank you. That was kind. How ever did you find me?"

"I simply asked the location of the most beautiful lady in Edinburgh," he said gallantly and Ishbel felt herself blush, unaccustomed to such comments, and heard a slight snort of disbelief from Harriette.

"MacPherson..." Harriette scrutinised him. "You are related to Lady Morrelly, I believe?"

"That is correct, Lady Huntly," he said, smiling, although there was a wary expression in his expressive eyes. "She is my aunt."

"And does she think it proper for you to gad about until the early hours of the morning, attending a court case surrounded by dissolute and disreputable characters?"

Mr MacPherson stared at her, clearly rendered speechless by such a rebuke from a complete stranger. Mortified and knowing the words were actually aimed at her, Ishbel exclaimed, "Harriette!" and glared at her.

Mr MacPherson glanced from one to the other of them then said, "The court case affected a great many members of society which is why so many attended the trial. I myself had my home robbed by Deacon Brodie, which is why I took such an unusual interest. Had you been there yourself I am certain you would have seen that no one would think the worse of your cousin for being in attendance."

Ishbel held her breath, knowing that Harriette hated being told what she should think; however her cousin's frown was now more curious than angry. "Would you care for a cup of tea, Mr MacPherson?"

"Er, yes, thank you." He looked thrown by this change in Harriette's attitude, as if suspecting a trap.

Harriette rang the bell for Gallach and told him to have afternoon tea brought in and they sat down to wait. Ishbel, perched on the edge of a stiff-backed chair, glanced at the grandfather clock. She could wait no more than twenty minutes or she would arrive late for the lecture and interrupt Professor Black, which would be unforgiveable.

"Will you be attending Lady Moreau's private ball on Monday?" Harriette asked Mr MacPherson.

"Yes, I shall. Will I have the pleasure of seeing the two of you there, My lady?" His eyes met Ishbel's as he spoke and his gaze was admiring. Other men had looked at her in that way but their interest had soon faded away once they learnt more of Ishbel's character so, even if she wanted to see more of him, there was no point in expecting it.

"Yes, we will both be there." Harriette smiled at Ishbel in a way that said there would be trouble if Ishbel did not agree to this.

Reluctantly and with annoyance, reminding herself that she owed Harriette this, Ishbel said, "I am looking forward to it." A superstitious chill ran through her as she wondered if she would be struck dead for such a complete lie, but of course nothing happened.

"Then would you allow me the honour of a dance?"

Ishbel swallowed against a sudden dryness in her throat. "I am not the best dancer."

"To put it mildly," Harriette agreed with feeling.

"Nor am I," Mr MacPherson said, ignoring Harriette's interjection, and continuing to gaze at Ishbel with a look of hope, as if her acceptance or rejection actually mattered to him. "Perhaps we could muddle through one together?"

He would regret this when he saw how graceless she was but she found she could not refuse him: "Yes. Thank you."

The door opened at this point and Gallach returned, supervising the footmen as they laid out the china tea cups and plates of shortbread. Ishbel's eyes darted once more to the clock. Ten more minutes. Harriette would be furious.

"The architecture of this house is beautiful," Mr MacPherson said to Harriette. The poor man was certainly trying his best to be amenable.

"Thank you. We are considering renting somewhere in the New Town but the building of the residential streets seems to be taking an unconscionably long time."

"I visited the New Town a couple of days ago," Mr MacPherson said. "The parks and streets are beginning to take shape. I believe, once the work is complete, it will add immeasurably to our great city's renown."

"You could be correct." The polite tone said that Harriette was undecided about Mr MacPherson but willing to give him a chance to prove he was not a complete fool.

They all took sips of their tea then Ishbel looked once more at the time.

"Are we keeping you from an urgent appointment, Ishbel?" Harriette asked in a deadly tone.

Caught, she could only make the best of it and explain. Mr MacPherson would think her a lunatic. "I apologise for my inattention. Mr MacPherson, I am sorry to cut short our meeting but I fear I must leave to attend a lecture." She watched his brow furrow in confusion.

"An appointment?" he suggested and she bit back a sigh.

"A lecture," she repeated. "Women are not allowed to enrol at Edinburgh University but we are permitted to attend lectures. I have not missed any of Professor Black's chemistry classes. Indeed, I spend much of my time at the College."

A long silence ensued and she could read the mix of confusion and surprise in those clear green eyes. Eventually, he said, "How interesting. Your education must mean a great deal to you."

It was the first time a gentleman had suggested something like that to her without intending it as condemnation. "Yes, it does."

"Then perhaps you would allow me to accompany you."

Now it was Ishbel's turn to flounder for a response. It was out of the question. What if he talked and interrupted Professor Black? What if he was condescending towards her fellow students or, even worse, towards Professor Black himself? It did not bear thinking about.

"What a wonderful idea," Harriette responded with a look that said this was Ishbel's fault and she would, therefore, have to deal with the consequences.

"Are you certain you would not find it dull?" Ishbel asked him.

Harriette interrupted. "I am sure Mr MacPherson knows his own mind." This was spoken with the irony of someone who has dismissed the majority of society as brainless imbeciles.

Mr MacPherson was once more looking from one woman to the other in a way that suggested he knew he was missing half the conversation but was not able to decipher the silent exchange. "I am sure I will find it most illuminating."

"There we are then," Harriette said, getting to her feet. "It is decided."

4. THE CASE OF THE MISSING NECKLACE

EWAN HAD not expected his first strong interest in a lady to be met with so little enthusiasm.

He mused on this, seated in his bedchamber, while his valet shaved him, keeping his head motionless as the deadly blade scraped at the skin across his jaw. He had thought at the trial that a mutual liking had sprung up between himself and Miss Campbell, or as much as was possible in their silent glances, but she had seemed more embarrassed than pleased when he had called upon her, although that could have been due to the presence of her intimidating cousin, Lady Huntly. However, in the four hours they were together in attendance at the university she seemed nervous and unhappy. He had done his best to be entertaining and to listen politely to the lectures – which had been intriguing in an incomprehensible kind of way – but the only time she showed any warmth was when he took his leave of her. Perhaps she simply did not like him.

He was sure most people saw him as a pleasant fellow, so her reaction was hurtful. Perhaps he should accept her behaviour as a dismissal but, on the other hand, he told himself she could have simply been exhausted after a sleepless night spent at Brodie's trial.

It was not simply her behaviour towards him that was unusual but that she should have a life spent attending university lectures and studying. Had she come from a poor or middle-class family then it would have made sense as he would have concluded that she wished to be a governess or school teacher but, coming from so grand and wealthy a family, she had no need to seek employment. While

Scottish gentlemen were more likely than their English counterparts to take on a respectable profession, it was unthinkable for a wealthy lady to do so.

Her peculiarities should cool his interest in her but instead he was more fascinated than ever. He wanted to understand her and hear more of her strange views of the world. Ewan was used to spending his time with men who talked of clothes, horses and gambling, and ladies who talked of dinner parties, balls and marriage. Ewan was a master at such conversations; with Miss Campbell, though, he was at a complete loss.

His valet had cleaned and put away the shaving knife now and was patting Ewan's face with a damp cloth. "Rabbie, in your honest opinion, do you find me to be an unintelligent man?"

"Of course not, sir!" Rabbie's response was reassuringly heartfelt and prompt. "Surely one of your friends did not say such a thing?"

"No, no one did. Or, at least, Lady Huntly hinted at it but I doubt anyone meets her favour so that does not trouble me. It is her cousin, Miss Campbell. The young lady studies extensively and I fear I have not made a good impression on her."

"I gather young ladies of that level like to be thought accomplished," Rabbie said as he put the bowl of water and damp towel to one side and picked up the cravat to affix around Ewan's neck.

"Not in this way. This is the seeking of knowledge to a degree I have never encountered before. She attends lectures at the university. Indeed, she is there so often that most of the students and professors greeted her by name."

"How bizarre. But you like her?"

"Very much."

"My oldest sister read novels for a while but then she married and gave up such nonsense."

"I learned to play the flute," Ewan recalled, "but lost interest after about a year."

Rabbie shuddered. "Yes, sir." He stepped back to survey the neckcloth then walked forward to adjust its folds slightly before moving away and Ewan bent down to pick up his orange-and-yellow waistcoat and put it on, doing up the gold buttons as he said, "I think I will call again on her and, if she still shows no pleasure in my company, then I will accept it and stay away. I will take some flowers and write a poem for her."

Rabbie twisted his lips and said hesitantly, "Don't you think that a lassie who has studied books..." He tailed off but Ewan caught where he was going.

"You think she might be critical of an amateur offering. Yes, you are right, it is better not to take that chance. I will just buy a bouquet of flowers."

Rabbie helped him on with his coat, ensuring that the lace of his shirt at the wrists was visible below the tight sleeves, although not too much as the current fashions demanded a less ostentatious style of outfit than previously. He slipped his stockinged feet into buckled shoes, accepted the tricorne hat Rabbie was holding out and was ready to leave.

His curricle arrived at Lady Huntly's residence at ten in the morning, a far earlier time than he would have usually dreamt of paying a call on someone, indeed an hour when he was often just beginning breakfast, but he had been led to understand that Miss Campbell often attended lectures in the morning as well as the afternoon. He wanted to be there before she left but, now he was here, he worried he might disturb the family before they were dressed.

He paused on the well-scrubbed steps before knocking quietly on the door. When a butler answered it, Ewan said, "I was hoping to see Miss Campbell but if the family does not usually admit visitors as such an hour then I can of course return later."

The butler gave him the blank look that seemed to be a requirement of the job and said, "Not at all, sir. Please come this way."

He followed the dark-clad servant through the hall and into a stately drawing room, which housed not just Miss Campbell but Lord and Lady Huntly as well. They were all seated on elegant, uncomfortable-looking chairs and Lord Huntly and Miss Campbell both held books while Lady Huntly had been sorting through calling cards. They got to their feet to bow or curtsy and Ewan bowed back and offered a smile. "I am relieved that I have not interrupted your breakfast."

"Good lord, no," said Lord Huntly. He was a man in his forties, his clothes smart but old-fashioned and overly plain. Ewan had seen him at various evenings out but Lord Huntly seemed to converse only with society's intellectuals so they had never spoken. "We are always finished before eight."

In the morning? No wonder Miss Campbell had some strange habits when coming from such an odd family. He held out the posy of flowers to Miss Campbell. "I saw these and their loveliness struck me as almost equal to your own."

She accepted them with a smile and murmur to gratitude, while Lord Huntly watched this with bemusement and Lady Huntly, with a sardonic gleam in her dark eyes. Miss Campbell rang the bell, requesting the servant to bring a vase of water for the flowers, then asked Ewan if he would care for a cup of chocolate or coffee.

"Chocolate would be pleasant, thank you."

They all sat down and Lady Huntly began asking him questions, less in the manner of making conversation than looking for a reason to eject him from her home. "Is Lady Morrelly well?"

"Very well, thank you."

"Do you have other family?"

"Just a married sister but she lives in London."

"Her husband is..?"

"Lord Picton, an English gentleman." He had not thought the man good enough for his sister and they had argued but she had been sure of her feelings, so he had accepted the marriage, wishing only that the couple had not settled so far away.

Lady Huntly said, "Are you acquainted with Lady Tinbough?"

The name was familiar but he could not bring to mind a face to match it. "No, My lady."

"She is a good friend of mine and I learnt yesterday that she has had an emerald necklace stolen from her. If you are planning on calling here on a regular basis then you can make yourself useful and find it for her."

Ewan thought at first that she was being humorous but her expression remained severe. The other inhabitants of the room looked as confused as he was. "How would I possibly find a missing necklace?"

"You found Ishbel," she pointed out. "Finding a necklace should be no more difficult."

"I obtained Miss Campbell's name and address by speaking to my aunt, Lady Morrelly. She knows all about eligible young ladies but I would be quite astonished if she knew the names of thieves."

"If you believe those two types of people are mutually exclusive then you are more of a fool than you appear."

Ewan had never encountered this level of rudeness in a lady before and was at a loss as to how to react. He looked to his host for inspiration but Lord Huntly had buried himself behind the latest volume of Edinburgh University's new Encyclopaedia Britannica at the start of the conversation and showed no sign of emerging from its depths. "You think the culprit could be a woman?"

"Of course. The thief most likely works in the house or visited it; a maid or someone invited to call. It could be a man but that seems less likely. I know Lady Tinbough and she has little enough patience for her husband; she would hardly encourage any other male attention."

He began to see the harmony of spirit that had caused Lady Huntly and Lady Tinbough to become friends. Unfortunately, he was also starting to realise that Lady Huntly shared her cousin's alarming intelligence since her assessment of the crime and its perpetrator was far in advance of his own. He did not see why she or Lady Tinbough could not solve the matter themselves but could hardly say so to a lady.

"Ishbel can assist you," Lady Huntly decreed and took a sip of coffee.

Ewan looked at Miss Campbell who accepted this with the same degree of consternation that must be visible on his own face. Although the task seemed an impossible one, he could think of no good excuse for refusing a request from a lady. "Very well."

As he and Miss Campbell looked at each other helplessly, Ewan thought that if this was the kind of work Lady Huntly set all her guests, then the household must receive very few callers.

5. THE HUNT BEGINS

"ARE YOU certain that Lady Huntly genuinely expects us to find the thief?" Mr MacPherson asked, regarding her with a degree of hope she fervently wished she could satisfy, for both their sakes, but Harriette never made requests without fully expecting them to be carried out. She would be scathing beyond all reason if they failed and, while Ishbel was used to Harriette's bad moods, she did not want to inflict them upon Mr MacPherson.

"Yes, unfortunately she does," she said and read the concern on his face. She shared it. Ishbel had always prided herself that she was intelligent enough to deal with any problem, but she had no idea how to find and catch a thief. They had come into the library to discuss the matter, Ishbel not bothering to call for her maid to chaperone them since she had no concerns about improper behaviour from Mr MacPherson. Amazingly, no one – meaning Harriette – had yet scolded her on this lack of propriety.

She took a seat on one of the rigidly upholstered chairs and automatically reached for a book, enjoying the solid, reassuring feel of it in her hands. Mr MacPherson sat down on the other side of a mahogany dropleaf table, turning the chair so he faced her.

"Then we should seek assistance from someone knowledgeable in these matters," he said. "There must be professional people who do such work."

"I believe one can advertise in the newspaper for what is called a thief taker but such people are usually criminals themselves and will make a deal that will get themselves and the thief the best reward."

She had heard talk of this dubious business at the university and could not see Harriette or Lady Tinbough agreeing to it. "Perhaps the Government employs similar people?"

"I know only of the Town Guard," he said with a grimace and she gave up on that idea. Even without their reputation for incompetence, the Town Guard did not hunt criminals down: they simply arrested people who were openly engaging in unlawful behaviour or whom others had caught.

"Then the matter is in our hands," she said, trying to sound confident, then she fell silent as she thought over the few details they knew so far about the crime. "I cannot agree with Harriette that the thief is likely to be someone employed in Lady Tinbough's home. As we both know, thieves are treated harshly by the law: branded, mutilated or even hanged. A working-class person with a good job would not be likely to risk so much."

"But look at Mr Brodie's actions," he said, brow furrowed. "People do not always act rationally or consider the possible consequences of criminal behaviour and an emerald necklace would be worth a fortune."

"Only if it could be safely disposed of which, surely, would be difficult for something so distinctive?" Again she was not certain where someone would sell a stolen item and the lack of knowledge was irritating.

"Who else could be the thief?" he asked. "A tradesman?"

"Perhaps but I think a member of society the most likely culprit…"

"Surely not!" he exclaimed, eyes widening at the idea.

"Someone from a respectable family – as Mr Brodie was – is far more likely to think they could get away with such a theft, that even if they were found out they would be let off with an apology whereas someone of lesser standing would face the harsh judgement of the law. There are certainly plenty of aristocratic families who have little money and high debts." Both ladies and gentlemen gambled to a degree that often shocked Ishbel, Harriette herself having once come home from a dinner party to announce that she had lost ten pounds at faro. Ishbel had said that such a sum could feed a working class family for a year, a fact which had failed to make any impression on her cousin.

"I suppose that is true," Mr MacPherson said. "Desperation might

26

make a respectable person do something foolhardy."

Ishbel was tempted to say that no upper class member of society knew the meaning of the word *desperation* when compared to what the working classes endured, working an average of fifteen hours a day in jobs that might destroy their health, but she did not wish him to think her as critical as Harriette and, in her experience, it was unlikely that he would mind about such things. Instead she focused on the matter in hand: the missing necklace. "Perhaps if we speak to Lady Tinbough we will find that there is a simple answer to this."

"Aye," he agreed with another of his engaging smiles. "That is an excellent plan."

6. LADY TINBOUGH

LADY TINBOUGH received them in the large, airy drawing room of her four-storey house. She was a woman of around forty – a few years older than Lady Huntly, Ewan would guess – who wore a purple dress covered in lace and ribbons and wielded her fan like a weapon.

"Harriette asked Mr MacPherson and I to call and endeavour to help find your missing emerald necklace, my lady," Miss Campbell explained in her quiet lilting voice. She sat with her hands clasped and a slight stiffness in her body, as though uncomfortable, which was not surprising given their strange role in coming here.

Lady Tinbough, by contrast, reclined in a theatrical pose on the chaise longue with a regal expression and a frown that seemed to be permanent. "How kind of Harriette."

"Would you permit us to ask you some questions about the necklace and when it vanished?" Miss Campbell opened a plain reticule and removed from it several sheets of parchment, a quill and ink. Ewan was beginning to think that she wrote about everything she encountered in life.

"Very well," Lady Tinbough said, as if bestowing a favour on them rather than letting them help her.

"Can you describe the necklace in detail?" Miss Campbell asked, leaning at a sideways angle – an uncomfortable-looking position that made Ewan smile – so she could rest her parchment on an ornate coffee table.

"The necklace has been in my family for several generations. It is part of a set with matching earrings." Lady Tinbough rang a bell and, when the butler came in, told him to tell her maid to fetch the earrings. The maid, a nervous-looking girl of no more than fifteen, arrived with the earrings a few minutes later and presented them to her mistress with a curtsy and, Ewan noticed, shaking hands. He did not know if that was a sign of guilt or fear but was inclined to think the latter. Would a thief have remained in the household? He thought not but perhaps the thief had known someone instantly leaving would be the first person suspected of the theft. If that was the case, they would have to possess strong will-power to face Lady Tinbough after committing this crime and he could not imagine the nervous maid capable of it.

Lady Tinbough waved the girl away with a sharp movement of her fan and handed one earring to Miss Campbell and the other to Ewan. Miss Campbell scrutinised the delicate object and leaned over, filling the silence with the scraping sound of quill on parchment.

Lady Tinbough glanced from her to Ewan, who smiled, and politely said, "The jewellery is lovely – delicate but striking and undoubtedly the highest quality."

Her frown retreated for a moment. "Yes. The necklace has some sentimental value to me..."

"Yes, of course," he agreed.

"... But that is less important than the fact that someone thought they could get away with stealing from me. That is unacceptable and I wish the thief caught and punished."

"Even if a member of society took it?" Miss Campbell asked, not looking up from her writing.

Lady Tinbough observed the profusion of red curls that were all that were visible of Miss Campbell's head. "I suppose that is a possibility. Yes, if the thief is from a decent family, I would want them publicly shamed for their behaviour."

Miss Campbell paused in her writing and glanced up briefly, a wry smile twisting rosebud lips, and Ewan remembered when she had said that a member of aristocratic society would never face criminal charges for the theft but a poor or middle-class person might hang for the crime. He had never considered such matters before but felt, through observing her reactions, a disturbing sense of injustice.

Miss Campbell lowered her head and the steady scratch of the quill once more sounded.

"Would you tell us when the necklace went missing?" Ewan asked.

"I wore it to a ball last week. Tuesday. I did not look for it until last night when I wanted it for Mrs Trent's musical evening and it was not in its case."

"Did your maid see it any time after last Tuesday?" Miss Campbell asked, looking over at the young girl who was fidgeting uncomfortably in a corner of the room by the door.

"Well, Ann, answer the question," Lady Tinbough ordered.

The girl shook her head, eyes on those of Miss Campbell, who was giving her a reassuring smile. "No, Miss."

"Did you see what happened to the necklace on Tuesday evening, Ann?" Miss Campbell asked.

"Yes, Miss. I unclasped it from Lady Tinbough's neck and took each earring and put them all in their case, as always." The poor girl gave a pleading glance at Lady Tinbough as she said this, as if she had already been blamed for the loss of the necklace and expected uniformed soldiers to burst through the door at any moment to arrest her.

"Yes, I do recall that they were put away on Tuesday night," Lady Tinbough acknowledged grudgingly and the maid seemed to start breathing again.

"Could you tell us the names of anyone who knew where the necklace was kept or might have been left alone in your room long enough to find it?" Miss Campbell asked. "Visitors? Tradesmen? Servants?"

"I find it difficult to believe that any of my servants would betray my trust in such an abhorrent manner," Lady Tinbough said, fanning herself. "I never employ anyone without thoroughly checking their background and morals. Ann is the only new member of staff, otherwise, the servants have all been in my employ for at least a year." She turned to her maid who dashed forward at the silent summons. "Ann, speak to the housekeeper and butler and find out if there have been any tradesmen admitted to the house in the last week and a half. If so, we will need their names and details."

"Yes, My lady." Ann curtsied and hurried out.

"I have admitted a number of people to my bed chamber, where my jewels are kept, for afternoon tea: Lady Huntly, of course; Mrs McRae, who usually brings her three oldest daughters; Mrs Abbott and her daughter; Lady Exton and her unmarried son and daughter; and His Grace, the Duke of Lothian. There might be a few others – it is difficult to recall who visited when, of course, my company is sought by a great many people, not all of whom I am at home to."

"Naturally," Ewan agreed, wondering how he and Miss Campbell could possibly question so many members of society about a robbery without offending them with the implication that they might be criminals.

"Do you know anything of your husband's visitors?" Miss Campbell asked.

"He is seldom at home," Lady Tinbough said shortly, confirming Lady Huntly's impression that they did not get along.

"Does anyone else live here?" Miss Campbell said.

"Just my son, the Viscount Inderly. He is, naturally, a popular and well-liked gentleman but none of his acquaintances would know anything about my jewellery."

"Could we briefly speak to him?" Miss Campbell persisted.

"If he is here, I will see if he can spare you a few minutes," Lady Tinbough said in a long-suffering manner and then the maid returned, bringing the butler with her and he confirmed that, no, the Viscount had not yet returned from a ride in the park with friends.

"I doubt he could tell you anything useful about this," Lady Tinbough said dismissively, then asked her butler about visitors.

"Naturally I supervise any unknown tradesman who is employed by Your Ladyship or His Lordship," he said, red-faced at being questioned over the matter, "but there were a couple of people who have worked here for a number of years, who I allowed liberty to carry on with their work: Pete, one of Mr Roberts' boys – a chimney sweep – and Mr McDougal, the carpenter, who repaired the broken library chair."

Miss Campbell wrote down the addresses of the work premises of the tradesmen, then thanked the butler in a polite manner that visibly soothed his discomfort.

"Sanders, Miss Campbell and Mr..."

"MacPherson," Ewan supplied.

"... Mr MacPherson will need to question all the servants about the theft of the necklace. I imagine it would cause the least inconvenience if they did so when Lord Tinbough and I are out, so perhaps tomorrow afternoon would be best. After three." She glanced at him and Miss Campbell for confirmation of this appointment.

Relegated to the position of unwanted tradesman, Ewan gave as courteous a smile as he could manage. "Of course, My lady."

Miss Campbell put away her writing materials and they left the house, pausing on the street outside, a large oak tree sheltering them from the brightness of the sun but not the excessive heat of the day. A coach pulled by two sleek black horses clattered past them.

"What an irritating woman," Miss Campbell observed as she put on a black wide-rimmed hat, drawing Ewan's eyes to her creamy skin and curls that were as bright as copper coins in the sunlight. "Anyone would think she was doing us a favour, not the other way around, and now I will miss a history lecture for this silly business."

"Indeed," Ewan agreed with a sinking sensation as he realised he would have to forego attending the birthday celebration of an acquaintance. His absence would not be missed by the host, Lord Judston, but Ewan had promised his friends, Chiverton and McDonald, that he would see them there.

"Oh, Mr MacPherson, I am so sorry," Miss Campbell said, looking at him with an embarrassed expression that caught his full attention. "I have no right to complain when I am at least helping a friend of my family but you have no duty here. If you wish to leave this business to me and return to your life..."

"Not at all," he quickly said, smiling at her. As much as he would love to walk away from this, he could hardly be so unchivalrous as to leave Miss Campbell in the awkward and potentially dangerous position of having to interview a group of people, including tradesmen, about a robbery. Anyone could take exception and turn violent. He wondered again how it was that they had become caught up in a matter so outside their normal life.

Miss Campbell was still looking up at him with an uncertain expression so he told her with more confidence than he felt, "We are in this together and I am sure we will swiftly find the culprit and the necklace."

7. AN EMBARRASSING BEGINNING

RABBIE, EWAN MacPherson's valet, was appalled to learn that his master had been imposed upon to do the same kind of menial work as a thief-catcher. Mr MacPherson was a society gentleman; he knew nothing of the real world nor the kind of people who inhabited it.

"It's like throwing a duckling into a nest of vultures," he told Simeon and Angus, the footmen, when Mr MacPherson had left to meet his friends for the evening. Betsy, the kitchen maid, darted about around them, putting out the cutlery and crockery for the staff dinner and the smell of cooking food wafted in and made Rabbie's stomach rumble.

"If he goes around accusing people of theft, he'll end up getting punched," Simeon predicted, sitting on the table, one polished shoe swinging back and forth.

"I'm sure he has more sense than to do that," Angus said in a doubtful tone and they exchanged worried looks.

"So is he likely to end up marrying this lassie who got him mixed up in all this?" Simeon stole a slice of bread, causing Betsy to tut him, and began munching on it. "If so, who knows what she'll involve him in next."

"He does seem taken with her," Rabbie said, reminded of this other difficulty. Were Mr MacPherson to marry poorly it would have a disastrous effect on the staff, who would then be under this odd woman's control. "She reads. Books. Not even novels, which is bad enough, but university books."

"Mr MacPherson knows nothing of books," Simeon said. "It will nae last."

"I believe he was not a bad scholar at school," Rabbie felt compelled to admit.

"But he has nae looked at a book since he left school, just as a sensible man shouldn't," Simeon insisted.

Rabbie forbore to mention that Mr MacPherson regularly read the accounts books for his estate, not wanting to damage his master's good name amongst the other staff. "I fear it will end badly."

"Aye," said Simeon while Angus just nodded his head and sighed.

Rabbie's parents lived nearby so he left to have dinner with them rather than at the house. The food was not as fine, but he liked to take the chance to see them regularly. He headed down the street in the direction of the Luckenbooths shops then took a side road and a rank-smelling alley to their street, greeting acquaintances on the way.

Rabbie had worked for Mr MacPherson for six years now and, from the start, had liked the easy-going gentleman but Mr MacPherson was sheltered at home and among his aristocratic friends from all the rough, violent things that went on in the world around him. He was kind to everyone, including his servants, but this whole nasty situation had made Rabbie see how someone could take advantage of the master or how he could get hurt. And what sort of lassie got a man involved in such a disturbing business? That was the result of books. It made people come up with daft ideas. The master should find himself a nice placid lass who did normal things and could settle him back in the comfortable world where he belonged.

Rabbie let himself into the family house and blinked a couple of times to get used to the dim interior, then headed through the plain unlit hall to the kitchen which was lit to an orange glow by both fire and a candle in the centre of the table.

"Did you wipe your muddy shoes on the mat?" his mother demanded.

"Aye, Ma."

"Well, dinnae stand there getting in my way. Sit down."

"Yes, Ma." He did so, then sniffed the air. "Is that a cherry pie?"

"It is." She smiled and, spoon in one hand, leaned over to pat his head.

He grinned at her and let the welcome thought of food distract him from his concerns.

Ishbel looked at her reflection in the full-length mirror in her bedchamber and gave a heavy sigh. The Robe de Cour was far too big and grand to suit her, with its mountain of gathered skirts and revealingly low-cut bodice, the whole concoction covered in lace and silly bows. Her hair had also been dressed in an elaborate style, pulled high above her head but with curls falling down behind her, powdered and decorated with large feathers. She looked ridiculous.

"You look lovely, Miss," her maid, Lucy, said firmly. "I am sure you will have a wonderful time."

"Lucy, I have never enjoyed a ball in my life!"

"This time will be different. Mr MacPherson will be there to dance with you and pay you compliments."

"Yes," Ishbel said, brightening. "We need to question the people who were in Lady Tinbough's house when her necklace was stolen. It will be different – I will have a useful purpose tonight."

Lucy's expression said this was not what she had meant but she ignored her. Ishbel had always felt like an insect pinned to a board and waiting to be dissected in front of all the critical aristocrats at balls. The women stood about making insults veiled in smiles and the men – from schoolboys to wrinkled old men – would stare at her chest and try to force her to dance with them. And if she managed to find someone from the College to have an intellectual conversation with, Harriette would drag her away, berating her about how unseemly it was for Ishbel to appear intelligent.

Holding the train of her dress so it would not trip her up, Ishbel left her room and walked carefully downstairs, the high heels of her shoes making her movements unsteady and her wide skirts barely fitting through doorways.

Harriette must have begun getting ready an hour before Ishbel as she was already waiting downstairs, Lord Huntly beside her and looking as excited about the ball as Ishbel felt.

Harriette examined Ishbel's outfit with lowered brows and a deep line across her forehead. "You are not wearing any makeup, Isobel."

"No," she agreed, ignoring the English version of her name her cousin insisted on using. Harriette's own face was painted white as well as having rouge over the cheekbones and a black beauty mark stuck in place, her gown even more elaborate than Ishbel's and coloured a deep wine red. The makeup and whitened hair made her look not quite human.

"We hardly ask much of you in return for the home and comforts we provide..."

Ishbel stiffened at the reminder that she was only here on her cousin's charity and had no home of her own. She dropped her eyes and swallowed. "Do you want me to go and put some makeup on?"

"No, there is no time," Harriette snapped. "Come along."

The evening was still light and warm as they descended down the front steps onto the street to the Huntly carriage, the family crest displayed prominently on each side. The residential street smelt of trees and flowers and Ishbel could hear birds singing. She thought longingly of just walking away, taking a stroll through the peaceful streets, then she dismissed the fantasy and let the footman take her hand and help her into the dim interior of the carriage, shutting the door behind her. She sat opposite Lord and Lady Huntly, facing backwards as the carriage lurched into movement.

Harriette gave her usual advice to Ishbel: "If any gentleman should actually wish to speak to you, keep your mouth shut and smile as often as possible."

Ishbel nodded meekly and, as usual, had not the slightest intention of doing as she was bid. Her goal was to speak about the robbery and find out as much information as possible. After that she would allow herself the respite of hiding in a corner and thinking about books. "Harriette, would you tell me something of Lady Tinbough?"

"I suppose I can do that." Harriette fanned herself in a measured way. "I have known her for all my adult life. She was born on an estate outside Edinburgh to an excellent family – she is niece to the Duke of Metherton and her brother, Lord Callen, is a well-known Whig and is friends with the Prime Minister. I do not know how she came to marry Lord Tinbough but she heartily dislikes him, his flirtations a source of embarrassment to her. They have one child and heir: the Viscount Inderly, a non-descript boy of marriageable age. She is an intelligent, well-respected member of society with a bluntness I find refreshing."

They arrived at their destination and the conversation ended. They had barely got inside the Assembly Rooms when she caught sight of Mr MacPherson and a moment later he saw her and headed over with two other men. He gave a wide toothy smile and swept down in a bow to them all. For some reason the sight of him filled Ishbel with relief, dispelling some of the butterflies in her stomach. He greeted them all warmly, then introduced his companions: Mr Chiverton was a handsome gentleman with a quick smile and courteous manners while Mr McDonald looked a little older, with pinched features and a more serious countenance. All three men wore formal outfits every bit as grand and elaborate as those of the women, Mr MacPherson resplendent in emerald velvet trimmed with silver and wearing a powdered wig for the occasion. The clothes brought out the vivid green of his eyes and he wore them with an ease Ishbel had never felt when wearing such ostentatious court outfits.

Harriette was waved over to another part of the room by some acquaintances so she and Lord Huntly left Ishbel alone with the gentlemen, unusual behaviour that either meant Harriette was sorry for her sharpness earlier or that she hoped with three men around her, Ishbel might finally find a husband. It was difficult to tell her reasons, but Harriette was not as heartless as she often seemed. At least, not all the time.

Eager to get to the work of the evening, Ishbel was disappointed when Mr MacPherson said to her, "I believe you promised to dance with me when I first called at your home."

Harriette's home, not hers, as she had recently been reminded. "I recall agreeing with the caveat that you would regret it when you saw how poor my dancing skills are."

"I could never regret time spent with so fair a companion."

"Then perhaps the minuet?" At least it would be the first dance so she could get the embarrassment out of the way.

"A perfect start to the evening."

She doubted he would think so for long. "After that we should really think of a way to talk to people of the missing emeralds."

"That is where my friend, McDonald, is useful," he said with a grin at the young man in question, who wore matching red silk coat and breeches with a red and gold striped waistcoat. "He is acquainted with Lady Exton's family and he can also introduce me to McCrieff."

"I do not recall that name," Ishbel said, confused.

"McCrieff is the Duke of Lothian."

"He is quite a gambler but that is a long way from accusing him of a scandalous robbery," McDonald said. He had a distinguished air but plainer features than his two friends.

"We will make no accusations without a great deal of proof," Mr

MacPherson promised.

"And where do you intend to get such proof?" Mr Chiverton asked.

Mr MacPherson remained silent, clearly having no answer for this, so Ishbel said, "Whoever the thief is, they must sell the necklace so we need only find who bought it and match that description with the person we suspect. Alternatively, someone might have seen somebody in Lady Tinbough's bed chamber or with the necklace and not realised the significance of what they saw."

Mr MacPherson smiled at her while his friends looked thoroughly taken aback by her speech, although she did not know why since it was all very obvious. Mr McDonald raised a quizzing glass to one eye to study her, which she disliked, so Ishbel was almost glad when the music started.

She placed her gloved hand in Mr MacPherson's as they stepped forward to take a place among the other dance couples. The problem with the minuet was that each couple performed their moves alone while everyone else stood about watching them so, if one did not do the dance well and Ishbel had not exaggerated her lack of skill, then everyone in the room would observe it. It was also far too long, so there was plenty of time to drag out the embarrassment.

At least Mr MacPherson could not tell how damp her palms were within her gloves although, from the reassuring look he gave her, he could feel the slight shaking in her hands that she could not quell. She focused her attention on him – instead of the sea of frowning faces – and began to move the steps, not letting herself think about anything but doing her part correctly. A couple of times her heeled shoes caused her to wobble and misstep but, as the music came to an end, she felt with relief that she should have done a lot worse. As she looked from Mr MacPherson's cheerful face to the room ahead of her, she caught sight of Harriette, who was watching her with an annoyed expression and shaking her head. Ishbel's confidence plummeted.

Mr MacPherson led her back to his companions when Mr Chiverton at once said, "Would you allow me to claim a dance later, Miss Campbell?"

Horror made her speak without thinking: "Mr Chiverton, you could not be so cruel to me!"

He laughed, amused rather than offended by her reaction, his two companions also smiling, so she was able to breathe again. "Since I have no wish to cause you distress, I will of course retract my request," he said, "but I hope you will at least believe me when I say that MacPherson did not exaggerate your beauty. Your presence here tonight makes the entire evening more enjoyable."

He certainly liked to employ the same false flattery as Mr MacPherson and, while she normally disliked the suggestion that her only purpose in a room was to look attractive, Mr Chiverton did not leer at her or speak in the intimate manner she had disliked in the past. Indeed, she could see the same amiable nature in him that made him wish to be kind to her as existed in Mr MacPherson and she found herself liking him.

"Shall we start talking to Lady Tinbough's visitors?"

"Certainly," Mr MacPherson said.

"But in the most tactful way possible," Mr McDonald stipulated.

"Of course, my friend," Mr MacPherson agreed.

They made their way through the crowd, past a group having an intelligent-sounding conversation on whether there would be a civil war in France which she would have liked to listen to. They finally reached a generously-proportioned middle-aged woman whose round face and narrow eyes were reflected in the features of four of the young men and women around her. Ishbel thought the group resembled a mother duck surrounded by feathered or, in this case, frilly ducklings. Mr McDonald made the introduction to Lady Exton and, by good fortune, Mrs Abbott's unmarried daughter was also with the group so that was four of Lady Tinbough's visitors all together.

"I believe we have an acquaintance in common," Mr MacPherson remarked to Lady Exton and, when she raised an eyebrow in question, he went on, "Miss Campbell and I had the pleasure of calling on Lady Tinbough earlier today."

"Aah, yes." Lady Exton studied him with more interest, such a connection apparently making him more eligible. "Do I know your family?"

"Lady Morrelly is my aunt."

"Yes, of course. I thought I had seen you with her. I have the greatest respect for that good lady."

Mr MacPherson smiled and Ishbel could see them never getting to the point if she did not intervene now. "We were shocked by what had happened to Lady Tinbough."

Lady Exton looked doubtfully at Ishbel, as if not entirely sure that she wished to know her. "What do you mean?"

"Have you not heard? She has had a valuable emerald necklace stolen within the last couple of weeks."

"How unpleasant," Lady Exton said.

One of her daughters added, "She must be furious. Where was it taken from?"

"Her bedchamber."

"Did the thief break in at night?" The daughter was wide-eyed at this thought.

"No, there was no break-in," Ishbel said, watching everyone's reactions. "The thief must have been someone who works at the house or a visitor."

"A tradesman," Mr MacPherson said quickly and Ishbel realised she had come too close to making an accusation. "We wondered if any of you might have spotted someone unsavoury acting in a furtive manner."

The younger women shook their heads while Lady Exton said coolly, "If we had seen anything of the kind then we would have informed Lady Tinbough at the time."

"Of course," Mr MacPherson agreed and, before Ishbel could say that they might not have understood what they saw, he changed to a different topic of conversation, then he and Mr McDonald led Lady Exton's unmarried daughter and Mrs Abbott's daughter onto the dance area.

Mr Chiverton was standing off to one side, talking about horses with Lady Exton's son, leaving Ishbel alone amongst the ladies who were viewing her with the disdain she had long since grown accustomed to. Lady Exton's haughty attitude made it difficult to believe she would commit a theft and the expensive clothes her whole family wore suggested no lack of money so Ishbel could think of no reason for any of them to commit the crime. Perhaps if she got to know more about them she might find a motive.

"Are you enjoying the season so far, My lady?" she asked.

"Somewhat," Lady Exton said, "but I always find these public balls to be over-crowded and full of a less than desirable type of person."

The cut was unmistakeable so, with burning cheeks, Ishbel

excused herself on the pretext of wanting to get something to drink. It was not entirely a lie as the Assembly Rooms were hot so she was thirsty but she still felt as if she were surrendering before having discovered anything useful and had failed Mr MacPherson. At this rate, they would never get anywhere with the investigation. Questioning people was not nearly as straightforward as she had imagined.

A servant handed her a glass of ratafia and she thanked him and took a sip, the sweet taste fortifying. Mr MacPherson had said he knew the Duke of Lothian so that left Mrs McRae and her daughters and it was up to Ishbel to find a way to question them.

She sought out Harriette who was talking with several of Edinburgh's wealthiest married women but broke off to glare at Ishbel. "Have you frightened off Mr MacPherson already?" she asked and her acquaintances looked amused.

Refusing to show that the barb had affected her, Ishbel said, "Are you acquainted with a Mrs McRae?"

"Yes, of course." Ishbel should have realised that Harriette knew everyone in society. "Why?"

"Would you introduce me to her? It is in connection with that matter you asked me to look into this morning."

"Very well." She gave her friends a look that said Ishbel was a useless child who needed to be looked after every second as she told them she would return shortly. As Harriette led her through the crowds of talking people all dressed in the finest silks and velvets, the orchestra adding to the noise, she said, "What are you up to?"

"Mr MacPherson and I are doing as you bid us," Ishbel snapped, wanting nothing more than to give up on the whole enterprise. "We are trying to discover who stole the necklace."

"If you think Mrs McRae or her daughters are responsible then you are vastly overestimating their wits."

"They might have seen the theft without realising it."

Harriette gave a wry smile. "That is entirely possible – I am sure a great deal happens around them that they fail to comprehend." She raised her voice and said, "Mrs McRae! How pleasant to see you here. Have you met my cousin, Miss Campbell?"

Mrs McRae and half a dozen young women curtsied to Harriette and Ishbel in a flustered manner and Mrs McRae asked Ishbel in a feathery tone, "Are you enjoying the ball, my dear?"

"Yes, thank you," Ishbel said with a smile, sorry for inflicting Harriette on the group and discomforting them all so thoroughly. "I had the honour of meeting an acquaintance of yours earlier today: Lady Tinbough."

This name brought more worried expressions, but Ishbel could not tell if this was guilt or simply that they found Her Ladyship nearly as intimidating as they found Harriette.

"I have not seen Lady Tinbough tonight," Mrs McRae said.

"I believe she might still be dealing with the blow of losing a very valuable emerald necklace. It appears to have been stolen."

They reacted, as the first group had, with some excitement at this piece of interesting gossip. Ishbel could discern no sign of guilt in them.

"Perhaps Deacon Brodie has escaped his prison cell to commit more dreadful crimes," one of the daughters suggested and got a frown from her mother.

"I fear this was no masked thief," Ishbel said. "No lock was picked so the thief must have either been working in the house or been a visitor to it."

"I presume you are not suggesting that I or one of my children might have been responsible for such a thing," Mrs McRae exclaimed angrily and there was a shocked silence.

"No, of course not. I just..."

But the group had already turned away, refusing to converse further with her.

Harriette shook her head and led Ishbel away, saying, "Did none of the countless dictionaries you possess define the word *tact*? You were supposed to find a necklace, not accuse everyone Lady Tinbough has ever met of the crime."

"We are doing our best," Ishbel insisted.

Harriette's expression made it all too clear what she thought of their endeavours.

8. OBJECTIONS

"EWAN, THIS is the Duke of Lothian," McDonald said. "Your Grace, may I introduce Mr MacPherson, Lady Morrelly's nephew."

Ewan bowed and smiled politely as he studied the impoverished duke, who was the only person they knew of so far who had a reason to steal Lady Tinbough's emeralds. He was a well-favoured gentleman of around thirty with black hair and dressed in the highest quality of clothes of a peacock blue colour. The duke nodded to him, took a swallow from what smelt like a glass of whisky and said cheerfully, "Aahh, yes, I knew your father slightly. Fearsome fellow – I expect he kept you in line."

"True, but I imagine it did me no harm," Ewan responded, recalling his father's stern nature and criticisms but reminding himself also of his strong sense of honour and duty. He had been an almost impossible man to please and had seemed to think he would live forever, never teaching Ewan anything about running an estate. It had been a difficult and lonely time after his death and Ewan's sister's departure to London with her new husband, but he thought he had managed his new job fairly responsibly. Focusing his mind on his current duty, Ewan said, "I had the honour of another introduction today – Lady Tinbough."

"Is she here?" The duke looked around. "I thought she had another engagement?"

"I met her earlier today when she mentioned..."

"Inderly!" The duke called out, waving over a thin, pale young man who approached them with a much older man. "Is your mother here tonight?"

So this was Lady Tinbough's son. The meeting could be a useful one, Ewan thought.

"No," Viscount Inderly said, "she is attending a musical evening at Lady Corchester's home."

"Oh, I thought you saw her here?" The duke said to Ewan, looking confused. The slight slurring of his words suggested he had had a good deal to drink.

"No, I met her at her residence. Lady Huntly had asked if her cousin, Miss Campbell, and myself would look into the theft of Lady Tinbough's emeralds," Ewan explained, glancing at the Duke who had no obvious look of guilt or other reaction to the words.

"Why on earth would my wife involve you in a purely domestic business?" demanded the man with greying hair who had joined them with the Viscount Inderly.

"Lord Tinbough?" Ewan guessed. "I am not sure whether or not we can help solve this but Lady Huntly merely wanted to offer assistance to her friend. I am an acquaintance of the family."

"I do not doubt that doing a favour for your betters seemed a clever move, but there is no mystery to uncover. My wife's necklace has been mislaid and I am quite certain it will turn up."

Ewan stiffened at this highly insulting comment on his motives and said, "If you wish Miss Campbell and me to withdraw our assistance then of course we will do so. Perhaps you could inform your wife..."

Tinbough cut across him: "Do what you like. I have no interest in my wife's melodramas." He turned and stalked away, leaving an uncomfortable group behind him.

"I apologise for my father," the Viscount Inderly said. "He and my mother had an argument tonight, but he should not take his bad moods out on everyone around him." His bitter expression suggested that he too had been subjected to Tinbough's rage.

"It is of no matter," Ewan said quickly. "Assuming your family does still want the necklace found, can you think of anyone who might have taken it?"

"No one. The idea of some thief breaking in is preposterous. As father says, it will very likely turn up having been put in the wrong case or something similar. It is kind of you to want to help but I trust you will not waste too much of your time on this."

"Why would Lady Tinbough imagine you could find a thief?" The duke asked, puzzlement in his eyes.

"An excellent question," McDonald said with a meaningful look at Ewan, before suggesting to the group, "Does anyone feel like a game of faro?"

"Yes, certainly," the duke said at once. "I am due for a lucky night, I can tell. Shall we refresh our drinks before starting?"

Ewan agreed, hoping that the duke might let something slip about the emeralds, whether he had taken them himself or seen anyone else, but this idea was quickly thwarted as several more people joined them at their table in the gaming room and the subject turned to the latest gossip of whose wife or husband had been seen with whom. The reaction of both Lord Tinbough and his son that the necklace had never been stolen also made him wonder if he and Miss Campbell were wasting their time. It would be a relief if they were and the necklace reappeared in a day or two's time, but he found he did not want to stop just yet. The puzzle was a distraction of sorts and it did allow him the opportunity to spend more time with Miss Campbell and find out more about her. She was the real mystery.

By the time the card game ended, it was around two in the morning and Miss Campbell and her family had already left. He was disappointed but he would see her again later in the day. She had looked enchanting tonight although the surroundings had seemed to leave her self-conscious and shy.

Chiverton, who had spent most of the night dancing, rejoined Ewan and McDonald towards the end of the night just in time to win every round he played and leave the house with them in a cheerful mood.

"We will see you this afternoon at Lord Judston's house," Chiverton said as Ewan's carriage pulled up to collect him.

"I fear not," he said. "I must interview servants with Miss Campbell about this theft business."

"Why on earth should you try to find the thief?" McDonald asked, frowning. "You have no possible abilities for such work and you are only succeeding in alienating people."

It was galling but Ewan could not help feeling McDonald's assessment was correct. He was blundering about with no idea what he was doing. "Lady Huntly placed the matter in the hands of myself and Miss Campbell," he tried to explain. "I cannot let Miss Campbell question servants and tradesmen on her own."

"She should not have to," Chiverton said. "The necklace stolen..."

"If it was even stolen!" McDonald interjected.

"... Did not belong to either of you so you have no obligations here," Chiverton continued, ignoring the interruption. "Just tell Lady Tinbough she will have to hire someone who knows how to deal with such matters."

"We promised to speak to Lady Tinbough's servants tomorrow – this afternoon, that is. I will meet Miss Campbell as planned and, if we make no progress with that, I will suggest backing out of this venture. If it is difficult for me then it is entirely unfair for Miss Campbell to be charged with such a task."

He opened the door to his carriage but was stopped by McDonald saying in a tone Ewan took offence to, "I trust you are not courting that young lady."

"Not at present, but I can think of no reason why anyone should object if I did."

"None at all, old fellow," Chiverton said, putting an arm round both their shoulders, and Ewan's anger faded.

"I simply meant that you could do better," McDonald said and Ewan glared at him, anger instantly returning. "You saw how gauche she was when dancing and her awkwardness talking to people."

"I found her a charming young lady and liked her a great deal," Chiverton said before an argument could begin, "but McDonald might have a point about her not being a good match for you. You know nothing of books and those kind of intellectual pursuits – none of us do. Our lives are taken up in different ways which, very likely, would not appeal in the least to Miss Campbell."

Ewan wanted to resist this argument. It hurt to be considered feeble-minded, although he knew that was not what Chiverton had intended to imply. He himself felt like an idiot in all the things he was ignorant of, in comparison to Miss Campbell's dedication to learning. When he had attended the university with her a couple of days ago he had only understood the tiniest fraction of the lectures they had listened to. In all likelihood she did need someone a great deal more learned than him but he liked her, although he still had no idea what her opinion of him was.

They would probably agree it best to give up this theft investigation this afternoon and then he would see where that left him with her.

"I need to get some sleep," he told his friends, abruptly keen to be away from them. "I expect I will see you in a day or two."

Chiverton clapped him on the back in a bracing manner and they took their leave of each other.

9. GOING ROUND IN CIRCLES

"I FEAR our questioning of possible suspects last night did not go as well as it might have," Ishbel said when Mr MacPherson came to collect her the afternoon after the ball. As she put on her gloves and hat in the hallway, she added, "I discovered nothing. Did you get anywhere?"

"No, but I did have an interesting meeting with an extremely hostile Lord Tinbough and his son, both of whom believe the necklace has been lost rather than stolen."

"They could be right," she said as the butler opened the door. As they walked out onto the steps, another less galling thought occurred to her: "Unless one of them had committed the theft and that was why they wanted us to stop looking into it."

"Why would a member of her family do such a thing?"

"I am not sure but, if you recall, Harriette said that Lady Tinbough did not get along with her husband."

"Lord Tinbough's attitude certainly seemed to confirm that. Why?"

"Perhaps he took the necklace out of spite or pique."

Mr MacPherson helped her into his curricle then jumped up beside her. "I also met the Duke of Lothian who said nothing of the theft but is a serious gambler. I have no idea if he would be devious enough to commit such a crime, but he should certainly remain a suspect."

"None of the women I spoke to showed any sign of guilt over the theft and I could think of no motive for them to have committed it.

The duke could be the culprit or someone who we have not yet thought of or the necklace might have simply been mislaid."

"This matter grows more convoluted by the day," he said as he got the two large white horses connected to the equipage to break into a trot. "I am beginning to think we should consider telling Lady Tinbough that she must hire someone with knowledge of how to pursue such matters."

"The servants might well have seen something," Ishbel said, not wanting to admit defeat so easily. It was a puzzle that she thought they ought to be able to solve. "They might at least be able to say whether Lady Tinbough often loses things."

"Let us find out," he said with a smile. "When will you next visit the university?"

"I attended four lectures this morning," she said.

He gave her a startled look. "You must have had to rise at a horrendously early hour."

"I breakfasted at seven-thirty as usual." She did not see why this should astonish him so and wanted to ask what time he normally arose, but the question seemed overly familiar.

"Do you think you will keep studying when you marry?" he asked, the question she had been asked at least two dozen times in the last few years sending a stab of irritation through her. He spoke more politely about it than many, but the implication was still that she was wasting her time and would only fulfil her duties as a woman when she married and bore her husband a male heir. Some men had said the words outright.

"I never intend to marry," she said.

"Why would you say such a thing?" he asked, turning a wide-eyed gaze on her.

"I am happy in my current life and have no interest in giving it up."

"I see."

There, it was said. Now he would vanish from her life just as men in the past had. It was better if it happened soon since she had been starting to like him.

They reached Lady Tinbough's elegant home and Mr MacPherson took her hand to help her down from the high perch with his usual courtesy and no sign of anger or offence, of which she was glad. Sanders, the butler, was, of course, expecting them and had arranged for them to question all the staff together in the servants' dining room. He led them down the hall past the drawing room, staircase, gaming room and parlour to a hidden staircase that took them down to the staff area which held the kitchen, pantry, butler and housekeeper's offices and their destination, the staff dining room.

Ishbel, who had been hoping to speak to people one at a time, looked at the dozens of people crammed into the room and had no idea where to start. She recognised Ann, the lady's maid, from their previous visit and Sanders listed the names and jobs of everyone else, each of the servants bowing or curtsying when their names were said. Ishbel memorised Mrs Fraser, the housekeeper, and Mrs Thomson, the cook but lost track of the others.

Sanders moved a chair back from the dining table for her to sit in and, thinking it might relax the staff if they were less formal, she sat down in it, Mr MacPherson sitting beside her, and she asked the staff to sit. There were less chairs than people, so places were taken by the senior members of staff and a few of the indoor people.

"As you know," Mr MacPherson said to them, "Lady Tinbough has had an emerald necklace go missing. Naturally she does not believe any of you are to blame, but she asked us to speak to you to find out if you saw anything helpful."

His diplomatic words had a noticeably calming effect and Ishbel was relieved. Some gentlemen – and ladies too – would have tried to coerce a confession out of these people and, knowing the kinds of difficulties working class people faced, Ishbel could not have allowed that.

"Did any of you see a tradesman or visitor in Lady Tinbough's bedchamber alone?" she asked and received blank looks and shaking heads.

"Had we any idea of the culprit we would have told Her Ladyship when we learnt of the burglary," the butler said with an expression that suggested he was embarrassed and distressed over the whole situation, his position as head of the servants and the person who oversaw any visiting tradesmen making it likely he blamed himself for what had happened. He was younger than her family's butler, perhaps forty, but had an air of authority, although it was dimmed slightly by the current situation. She did not suspect a man in so good a job of the theft but thought he was probably the person who knew all the servants best, although if he had had any serious suspicions she believed he had spoken truthfully in saying he would have spoken to Lady Tinbough about them.

"You mentioned a couple of tradesmen," Mr MacPherson said. "Do you believe either of them could be the thief?"

"I find it unlikely, sir. The chimney sweep boy is far too timid and well-behaved to dare do such a thing and the carpenter has visited the house countless times. Besides, neither of them would have any idea where Lady Tinbough kept her jewels."

That was a good point, Ishbel thought. "Is there anyone you do think a likely culprit?"

"Certainly not the staff. I cannot imagine anyone except a professional thief daring to do such a thing."

There were a few nods at these words and no one else spoke up.

"Is there any way a stranger could have got into the house without breaking in?" she asked.

"No, miss. It would be impossible for a stranger to get past all of us unseen during the day and all the doors are locked at night."

That led them back to the beginning, with no idea who to suspect. She glanced hopelessly at Mr MacPherson who gave a slight shrug of his shoulders.

"Is there any way that this could not be a theft? Does Lady Tinbough ever lose items?"

"No, miss," said Ann, the slender lady's maid they had met on their last visit here, who was one of the youngest members of the staff. She blushed as she spoke and her quiet words were difficult to hear. "That is, her ladyship sometimes says 'where is such-and-such?' and it takes a few minutes to find something she's put down in a different place, but I searched everywhere for the necklace. I checked through every drawer and jewel case in the room."

The housekeeper, an attractive woman of about thirty with an eloquent manner, said, "I helped Ann search the room again and Mr Sanders had the footmen go through the rest of the house."

"The necklace is nowhere in the house," the butler agreed.

"Is there anything else you want to ask?" she checked in an undertone with Mr MacPherson and, when he answered in the negative, she said aloud to the group, "We appreciate you all taking the time to speak to us and apologise for disrupting your day with this unpleasantness. Should any of you remember anything that might point at a suspect then I know you will inform Lady Tinbough or have a message sent to us."

As Sanders led them back up to the hall, Ishbel said to him, "Is there anyone in the staff you think could be capable of this? You may speak any concerns to us – we will certainly not accuse anyone without proof."

"I know all the servants, Miss Campbell, and I am certain none of them committed this crime."

She nodded. "I think it unlikely too. Thank you."

He opened the door for them and, as they got out onto the tree-lined street, Mr MacPherson turned to her and said, "I fear we must tell your cousin that we cannot continue with this. We have made no progress and, frankly, I would not have a clue what to do next."

She wondered if his words were entirely about the theft or whether her confession that her studying meant more to her than marriage was part of his desire to end his association with her. Either way, she had no right to waste any more of his time. She told herself she would be glad to put the matter behind her and get back to her education but, in truth, she disliked this sense of failure. He wanted it over, though, so there was nothing else to be done. "I will inform Harriette."

"I will accompany you," he said.

"You need not."

"I wish to," he insisted, as chivalrous as ever and she felt a stab of unhappiness at the idea that this might be the last time she ever saw him.

They returned to the Huntly house and found Harriette in the hot kitchen below-stairs, supervising the cooks as they made jam. Since Ishbel was confident that the cooks were more than capable of managing on their own – and would indeed be the happier for Harriette's absence – she had no qualms in asking her cousin to come to the drawing room to speak with them. Mr MacPherson awaited them there and, at the sight of him, Harriette said, "Does this meeting mean that you have found the missing necklace?"

"I fear not," Mr MacPherson said and Ishbel fought back a sudden urge to stop him continuing. "Our questions have brought no answers..."

"... No, the two of you merely seem to have offended a great many people."

Given Harriette's propensity for being offensive, this was difficult to take and Ishbel did not want Mr MacPherson to have to face her cousin's scorn. "Since we do not know how to conduct such an investigation," Ishbel said, "it would clearly be better if Lady Tinbough hired someone professional to look into it."

"Very well. I had thought your self-proclaimed intellect and Mr MacPherson's... well, whatever qualities he has... would have made this a simple task for you to accomplish. If it is so far beyond your abilities that you are beaten so quickly, then, as you say, Lady Tinbough will be forced to hire less trustworthy persons to do it."

She bestowed a look of contempt upon them both then swept out of the room.

After a long mortifying silence, Mr MacPherson said, "I believe, should you be willing, that I wish to continue looking into the robbery."

"Yes. So do I."

10. GETTING HELP FROM THE VALET

"WE SHOULD discuss what tactics to employ next," Ewan said as he and Miss Campbell sat opposite each other in the drawing room of her house. Not only was he stung by Lady Huntly's rebuke, but he felt she had been monstrously unfair to Miss Campbell. The only solution to prevent Miss Campbell being subjected to further criticism was for them to solve the theft. Somehow.

"I wish we had been able to speak to the servants individually," she said with a furrowed brow. "I cannot believe no one saw anything of what happened. They might simply not have realised the importance of what they saw."

"They might speak more freely to someone of their own class," he mused, an idea coming to him. "What if I sent my valet into the household on the pretext of seeking a job? He might have better luck than we did?"

Her expression brightened. "That is an admirable notion." She gave him a dimpled smile and his entire day was brightened.

"I will return home and arrange it and Rabbie, my valet, can come here to let us know what he finds out."

"Would it not be easier for me to visit you to hear from him?"

He stared at her, shocked she would suggest such a thing. "I am an unmarried man. It would ruin your reputation to come to my home."

"Oh, yes," she said as if she had forgotten this fact. "I have a lecture to attend in half an hour but will be home in less than two hours then I will be in all evening so you and your valet may call any time then. Will you stay and have dinner here? Harriette and Lord Huntly will be here, but they have no guests coming so it would be informal."

"I would be honoured," he said and bowed to her. She gave a curtsy in response and he left the white-brick house. He wondered what kind of people her parents had been that they should have failed to make clear that it was vital her reputation be spotless. He shuddered to think of the kind of gossip and snubs she would have faced had she ever been seen at his home. A gentleman could survive such things – although he would have been labelled a cad for destroying a young lady's reputation – but she would have been cut from fashionable society forever.

He thought again of what she had said in the curricle about never wishing to marry. His instinctive reaction had been to assume she was being kind and had instead meant that she would never consider marrying him. Perhaps, however, she had been telling the exact truth and was unconcerned about other people's opinions of her because she intended to remain a spinster. The whole idea bothered him: he was not yet sure that he wished to marry her, but he certainly liked her better than any other woman he had ever met. Why would anyone – other than Chiverton and those of his inclinations – refuse the possibility of marriage? It made no sense to him, especially as Miss Campbell's life, living in the harsh company of her cousin, must be far from paradise. Did not everyone want a companion to lean on and save them from loneliness?

He was tempted to call at his aunt's house and ask her about Miss Campbell's background, but that seemed a little underhand. While such a conversation was rather personal, Miss Campbell was sufficiently unconventional that he did not think she would take offence at his asking a little more about her reasons for wishing to stay unmarried.

He rode his curricle round to the stable at the back of his house, left the horses to be taken care of by his groom and headed inside. As always, his butler, MacCuaig, met him in the hall to take his hat and gloves so he asked the older man, "Is Rabbie about? I want to ask him something."

MacCuaig frowned at the informal way he spoke of his valet. "I will send Camran to your room to serve you as you wish, sir."

"Thank you." Ewan headed up the sweeping staircase to the

master bedchamber and selected evening clothes to change into later for when he called back at Miss Campbell's house. He wondered how Lady Huntly would react to the news that her cousin had invited him for dinner there. He hoped she would not say anything unpleasant and upset Miss Campbell. Anything else. He was still smarting from her earlier put-down.

Ewan turned at a sound behind him and found that his valet had arrived and was looking at the clothes laid on the bed.

"Do you wish me to help you change, sir? It is a little early for formal wear."

"Those are for later. I am invited to dinner with Miss Campbell's family. No, I wanted to talk about something more important than clothes."

Rabbie stopped short and stared at him. "More important?" he said in a quivery tone.

Realising his blunder, Ewan corrected himself. "Of course, one's clothing is extremely important. What I meant to say was that this was something else equally important. I have a favour to ask."

Rabbie visibly relaxed and made an expansive gesture. "Anything, sir."

"It is about this robbery I am looking into..."

"... Are you quite certain these people are not taking advantage of your kind nature with this business, sir? It does not seem like something you would willingly choose to do."

That was entirely accurate and, therefore, a question best avoided. "Do you think Miss Campbell and I cannot find the thief?"

"I think it's outside of the things you know about and could be dangerous."

"That is precisely why I cannot allow Miss Campbell to look into it alone."

Rabbie frowned. "It is certainly not fit work for a well brought up lady, sir, but that does not mean either of you should be involved in it. None of us would be happy if you were hurt. Nor if any more of your clothes were ruined."

Amused at the man's priorities, he said, "I appreciate that, Rabbie, but I believe we will surprise you all. We just have to find the right approach."

"Aye, sir," the valet said, regarding him with a deeply worried expression.

"You are very welcome to refuse this if you wish. I would certainly not hold it against you."

"What is the task, sir?"

"I would like you to go to Lady Tinbough's household with the excuse that you are seeking work and see if anyone will talk to you about the robbery. Anything you could find out would be useful but, as I say, if you would rather not do it then that is fine."

"I can do that, sir."

They discussed what sort of things the valet should ask then, Ewan having double-checked that Rabbie really did not object to this employment, the young man set out.

Miss Campbell would not yet be back from the university, so Ewan took his time washing and getting changed. It took him a dozen tries on his own to get his neckcloth tied with any degree of elegance, so it was lucky he was not in a hurry.

As he sat down to put on his polished silver-buckled shoes, he thought about Rabbie's comments earlier as well as those of his friends last night. None of them seemed to believe he should be doing this task and Chiverton and McDonald both thought he was not sufficiently intelligent to suit Miss Campbell. Was he really such a fool? It was true that he had not achieved anything remarkable in his life so far, but he lived in a similar way to most other wealthy men of his age. He had always supposed that if there was something he really wanted, whether a profession or acquiring a new skill, that if he worked hard he could achieve it. Now he began to doubt himself. He thought of asking Miss Campbell her opinion but did not want to put her in the awkward position of having to say that, yes, she did indeed think him dim-witted.

Ewan had attended the boys' grammar school here in Edinburgh when he was younger. He had not excelled but he had not failed any of his classes and it had not been a case of him struggling to understand his lessons but, rather, a youthful lack of interest. If he wanted to impress Miss Campbell – and he found that he did – then he needed to show her he could pursue this theft business in an intelligent, methodical manner. He would do everything in his power to track down the thief.

11. RABBIE'S NEWS

RABBIE, FRANKLY, had no idea what he was doing, but he had no intention of letting the master down, so that was all there was to it. He found the house Mr MacPherson had described to him and it was even bigger and grander-looking than his own workplace. He wished he had stopped at a tavern for a snifter to give him the courage to go through with this, but it was too late now and, anyway, the staff might not take to him if he had the smell of liqueur on his breath. He walked round the side of the house to the tradesman's entrance and knocked on the door.

Five minutes later, after a sob story he could hardly believe had come from his own lips, the butler had invited him to join the staff for dinner and he was led into good-sized room where the staff were just about to begin the meal. He repeated his fictional tale of loss and hardship as he wondered if any of them was a thief.

They were a good-natured lot, even the butler, which in Rabbie's experience was unusual. The footmen were both a bit older than Rabbie's work colleagues so presumably they had been here for some time and they both seemed friendly enough. There were a few young women, all a bit shy of him, and a couple of older ones he took to be the cook and housekeeper. No one had the shifty look of a thief. Besides, if one of them had taken something so valuable as an emerald necklace surely they'd have scarpered and be in England by now?

"Have you all worked here a long time?" he asked.

"Ann is new," the butler said, indicating a young lassie.

"And what is your job, Ann?"

Blushing furiously and looking no higher up than his shoulders, she said, "Lady's maid, sir."

He studied her with interest. She was the only one who would have handled the necklace regularly and had the best chance of taking it unseen but she would also be the first person suspected. She was certainly the last person he would imagine being a thief. She was no older than his little sister, May, who had just turned fifteen. The girl had a washed-out look: pale blonde hair; pale complexion; of average height but with a skinny, underfed bony appearance. "That must be nice – Her Ladyship must have beautiful clothes."

"Yes, sir."

"Are the lord and lady kind people to work for?" At once everyone was avoiding his eyes and the conversation briefly died.

The butler said firmly, "We have no complaints."

"Of course not," he agreed, wondering about the reactions. "A job in a good house like this is hard to get. I should know."

"Quite so."

"Did any of you follow the trial of William Brodie?" he asked. "What a shocking business, deceiving people like that."

"There has been some unpleasantness of that nature in this house," the housekeeper said. She was young to be running a place like this and had a posh accent, suggesting a middle-class family that had run out of money, forcing her to get a job. "The mistress has had a necklace stolen."

"Aye." The butler took a swallow from his glass of ale. "And none of us are exempt from suspicion."

"How nasty for you," Rabbie said. "Who do you think could have taken it?"

Ishbel had only been back in the house for five minutes when Mr MacPherson arrived. She had been impressed by his idea of getting his valet to visit Lady Tinbough's household and had tried to come up with some strategies of her own, only to find that she had missed most of the lecture and only thought of the obvious next step of visiting the tradesmen who had called at Her Ladyship's home.

She stood to curtsy when the butler led him into the library then almost forgot to do so, distracted by how well his evening clothes suited him. She had not yet grown used to how attractive he was and it was disconcerting.

After bowing to her he said, "My valet agreed to the subterfuge and will come here as soon as he finds anything out."

"Good."

They sat down and he said, "What was the subject of your lecture today at the university?"

She was warmed at his interest. Even her fellow students at the College had always seemed bewildered at the idea that she could share their love of learning, it being so ingrained in them that women could not have the intellect nor desire for such things. The men were used to her now, but she knew that they would always think her strange and if they could not appreciate how she felt that she had believed no one could. "Materia Medica," she answered him. "Professor Home discussed the plants that would be used to make medicines to treat a fever." She had sufficient books on the subject that she could write up what she had missed due to her inattentiveness.

"If you do not mind my asking, do you have any relations who are – or were – academics?"

"My father taught chemistry at the College and of course Lord Huntly is a professor there teaching Latin."

His startled expression suggested he had not known about Lord Huntly's profession but what he said was, "Did you get your love of learning from your father?"

"Yes, I think so. I sometimes sat at the back of the room and listened to his lectures as a child." She had fallen in love with the whole world of academia, everything from the smell of the books to the way it made her see the world as far more extraordinary than she had previously known.

"That must have pleased him."

"No." The memory came to her of her father's sharp words and the bruising grip of his hand on her arm whenever he caught her there. "He... He wanted other things for me."

"And what did your mother want?"

"I have no idea. I barely knew her."

"She died when you were young?"

"No." She had just never had the slightest interest in Ishbel. "My father died first and she caught the consumption from him and died within two months of him. I was fourteen. Harriette and Lord Huntly have allowed me to reside with them since then, so I have been fortunate."

"My mother had been ill for years before she died," he told her and she leaned forward to listen. "I was thirteen, but I still miss her – I miss all of them. My father had a heart attack when I was seventeen."

"You said *all of them* – did you have other family you lost?"

"No. Well, not in that sense. I had – have – an older sister, Matilda, I used to be close to but she married before my father's death and has been living in London ever since. I must confess I felt very alone when he died and I inherited the estate – I had no idea how to run it but luckily I have an excellent manager who helped me learn everything I needed."

"It must be a lot of work," she said, seeing him in a new light as she realised everything he had had to deal with. It touched her that he would share this.

"Not really. Mr Insch handles all the day-to-day work. I only need to make a decision when there is some larger matter to deal with."

There was a lot more she wanted to ask but the butler entered to say in a distressed manner, "There is a *person* by the name of Camran who is insisting on speaking to you, Miss."

"Yes, we are expecting him," she reassured Gallach. "Please show him in."

"Yes, miss." With every sign of reluctance, he led in a young, well-dressed but unmistakeably working-class lad who grinned at Mr MacPherson and was responded to in kind.

"Thank you, Gallach," she said and, as he departed, she let Mr MacPherson introduce her to his valet.

"We are very grateful to you for helping us with this matter, Mr Camran," she said to him.

"Did you discover anything interesting, Rabbie?" asked Mr MacPherson.

"Aye, sir. I think I might have worked out who the thief is, although I don't know how you'll catch the culprit."

12. THE MISSING MAID

"WELL, THE staff think one person is the thief and I think it's another," said Rabbie Camran, the valet.

"Perhaps you should have a seat," Ishbel told him, "and tell us everything from the time you arrived."

"Thank you, Miss." They all sat down and she saw his eyes dart round the library, taking in bookcases, velvet curtains and books on every available surface, including the floor. Then he focused on his master and began to speak. "I asked about work, as you said, and acted a bit hungry so they'd take pity on me. They said a suitable job might well come up soon, so I know where to go if you kick me out, sir." This last comment was made with another grin and Mr MacPherson laughed. She too smiled, glad to see a gentleman treating a servant like a real person and not expecting constant subservience. It occurred to her that she had not yet discovered anything she disliked in Mr MacPherson.

Mr Camran went on: "The staff let me have dinner with them and I asked if they had heard the verdict over Mr Brodie. They reacted as I hoped with the housekeeper bringing up the theft of the necklace then the general maid said she knew exactly who had taken it, but the butler shushed her at once and said she would lose her job saying such things without proof about a gentleman. She went quiet and the lady's maid – the first lassie who'd spoken – was talking about being new to the household herself but that she was fairly paid. She was saying that because of what I'd said about getting a job there..."

"Yes, but what about the thief?" Mr MacPherson prompted.

"But that's who I think it was."

"The maid?" Ishbel asked, confused as to his reasoning.

"Aye. She just vanished. It was before the robbery took place but, because she knew the household and all the corridors and back stairs, I'm sure she could have sneaked into Lady Tinbough's room without being seen."

"Who are you talking about?" Mr MacPherson asked, confusion that matched hers in his expressive eyes.

"The maid who this new lassie replaced. She worked in the house for more than a year, then a week before the robbery she just disappeared. No letter of resignation. None of the staff even saw her go. She had a bedroom in the annex and, when she didn't show up for breakfast one day, someone went to fetch her and all her clothes were gone and there was no sign of her. She must've split in the night, they reckon."

"What makes you believe her to be the thief?" Ishbel asked.

"Well, the timing, Miss. Someone must've upset her to make her leave in that way and if that person was Lady Tinbough then she would've had a grudge. She could've gone back to get the necklace out of revenge and the need for money."

"Working in the house, she would have known where the necklace was kept," Mr MacPherson said.

"Did you find out her name?" Ishbel asked, grabbing a fresh piece of parchment from a stack and unstoppering the bottle of ink.

"Aileas Jones, Miss."

"Thank you," she said as she picked up a quill. "That was very well reasoned."

"Yes, well done," Mr MacPherson said enthusiastically, then paused and added, "but what of this other suspect? You said the lady's maid thought a gentleman was the thief?"

"Aye, sir. I managed to ask her about it before I left. She thought the Duke of Lothian was responsible. Apparently he was at the house all the time, telling all the ladies and gentlemen how broke he was."

"But he could not possibly have known where the jewels were kept," Mr MacPherson pointed out and she liked hearing the intelligent way he viewed matters now he was taking the case seriously. He was like a different person.

"That's not true, sir. The lady's maid said he had been in Lady Tinbough's bed chamber with a couple of other people when Her Ladyship was putting on the necklace for a ball. The maid was certain he had seen where it was kept."

"Then either one of them could have done it," Ishbel said, writing the duke's name below that of the missing maid.

"My money's on the girl," Mr Camran said. "She had a reason – if Lady Tinbough was unkind which, I gather, is sometimes the case – and she would have found it easier than a duke to sneak about unnoticed. Besides, would a duke stoop to stealing a necklace?"

Ishbel put down the quill and stoppered the ink, surprised that he should have a higher opinion of the upper classes than she did.

"If he was badly enough in debt," Mr MacPherson was saying, "he might have taken advantage of a visit to the house to steal. I think we should look into both possibilities."

"I agree," Ishbel said, her mind on the maid. Something must have distressed her a great deal for her to leave without a word in the middle of the night. If she had committed the theft perhaps she had been desperate. Even if she had done it out of anger, the possibility that she could hang for the crime was unacceptable.

If the maid was the thief then they had to find a way to help her.

13. MARRIAGE ADVICE

"I CAN see now why you're so smitten with Miss Campbell, sir," Rabbie said, helping Ewan into his coat the next morning. "She isn't how I expected her to be."

"I am not smitten, Rabbie." Ewan stood still as his valet checked his outfit and made a few small adjustments to it. "So what did you expect her to be like?"

"A lot more serious. She was much more friendly and much prettier than I'd thought, although you can tell she's smart. You could certainly do a great deal worse."

"I am working with Miss Campbell, not courting her and you say that as if you expect me to choose someone unsuitable."

"I do if you're going to use a word like that. That's a weak, insp... ins..."

"Insipid?" Ewan suggested, sitting on the bed so Rabbie could help him get his boots on.

"Yes. It's an insipid word meaning someone that suits everyone else, but you don't feel any passion for her. There's no point in marrying someone who doesn't set your blood on fire."

"So, in your great experience of marriage..."

"I may be a bachelor like you, sir, but I'll know when I meet the right lassie and she can be as unsuitable as she likes as long as she turns my head until I can't see anyone else."

With these words in his ears, Ewan headed downstairs. He was not surprised that Miss Campbell had made such a good impression on Rabbie. For some strange reason, she seemed more comfortable talking with working class people than her own set – she had been confident, the charming woman he had always found her to be, talking to Rabbie whereas, at the ball the evening before, she had been nervous and uneasy, as if constantly expecting criticism. He frowned, wondering if this was Lady Huntly's doing.

In the hallway his butler held out his hat and gloves.

As Ewan put them on he said, "MacCuaig, could one of the footmen be spared for the morning? I want him to do some asking around for me about a missing maid."

The lines in the butler's forehead deepened and he pursed his lips. "Of course, although if sir wishes the staff to be put to such uses in the future, perhaps he would like me to hire some miscreants for that purpose."

Ewan ignored the sarcasm. "You can send him into the dining room for instructions."

He headed into the room and was quickly joined by Angus Smith, who had been a footman here for about five years and was only slightly older than Ewan. Angus seemed to have adopted MacCuaig's liking for blank expressions but, thankfully, had not yet caught his sarcasm. Ewan told the footman what Rabbie had discovered and asked if he could try to find out more about the maid. "I will be in this afternoon so if any of the caddies know anything of her would you send them to talk to me?"

"Of course, sir."

"Thank you, Angus."

He left the house, walking the familiar route to the main shopping area with its mix of shops, stalls and a few people selling flowers and other light items from a basket.

He thought over last evening as he strode along, a cool breeze reducing the August heat. He had not had the chance to ask Miss Campbell if she had been joking about never marrying and it was something that was still on his mind, bothering him. On the other hand, he was not utterly certain yet that he wished to court her, although his feelings grew more fixed by the day, so perhaps it would have given an unfair impression to have raised the subject again. It would be unthinkable to make her anticipate an offer from him that he then failed to make. Of course, it would also be highly unpleasant for him to decide to make her an offer that she had no interest in even considering.

The discussion about their families had intrigued him, leaving a lot unspoken. It sounded as if she had not had a particularly affectionate relationship with either of her parents. And now she lived under the roof of Lady Huntly. No wonder Miss Campbell sometimes had a pensive air. Perhaps that too had something to do with her attitude to marriage, making her wary of letting anyone get close to her. That would fit with what he knew of her.

He reached his tailor just in time for his appointment on the important matter of a new outfit, the comments about the waistcoat becoming quite heated before a decision was reached for it to have vertical green and purple stripes.

He left there with a sense of great accomplishment and, on a whim, then entered a bookshop and purchased a number of medical books that the seller assured him were appropriate for a novice.

He returned home and took his new purchases into the parlour, glancing through the books over a glass of whisky before settling on the one that had illustrations. As he turned the pages he became increasingly concerned, on Miss Campbell's behalf, at how many of the pictures – for the purposes of explaining muscles and bones – showed naked male bodies. Surely the professors at Edinburgh University would ensure she was not subjected to images that must surely disturb an innocent lady?

As he was worrying about this, his second footman entered the room, having completed his errands on Ewan's behalf. Ewan closed the book and put it on a coffee table, giving Angus his attention. "How did you get on?"

"Only one of the caddies knew the maid by sight and said he would keep an eye out for her, but I couldn't find any sign of where she is now. I got the name and address of her parents if that helps at all."

"It does indeed. That is excellent work," Ewan said, walking over to his writing desk and getting out parchment, ink and quill to write down the information. He should call on Miss Campbell as soon as possible to share this.

14. A DIFFERENCE OF OPINIONS

ISHBEL ATTENDED lectures all day and returned to the Huntly residence in the early evening to find Harriette entertaining Mr MacPherson or, more likely, entertaining herself at his expense. Mr MacPherson relayed what his footman had learnt which they agreed gave them another avenue to pursue and it was heartening to hear that a caddie was searching for Aileas Jones for them. She felt they were at last making real progress.

Since Harriette showed no sign of leaving them alone, Ishbel decided to make use of her knowledge of society. "What do you know of the Duke of Lothian?" she asked. "Specifically, just how badly in debt is he and could he be our thief?"

Harriette leaned back on the chaise longue with a rustle of silk and petticoats and began to fan herself. "He comes from a distinguished family and has not only gone through a considerable fortune but also frequently gets into debt that he cannot pay off. At the start of the week he bought a matching pair of bay geldings to pull his new phaeton."

"Where did he get the money for all that?" Mr MacPherson asked.

"No one knows but, if you intend to ask him if he stole Lady Tinbough's necklace, you should be careful as he has a quick temper and takes pleasure in fighting duels."

"Perhaps I should speak to him," Miss Campbell suggested. "He can hardly challenge me to a duel."

"You could charm him into telling you about his life," Harriette suggested and, for some reason, the words made Mr MacPherson breathe in sharply, straightening in his chair.

Ishbel could not tell if her cousin was mocking her or not. "Could I?"

"Certainly not," Mr MacPherson insisted in an unusually firm tone. "That would be a horribly awkward situation to put your cousin in, Lady Huntly."

"I do not see why," Ishbel said, hurt that he did not think her capable of doing this. "I may not be competent in large social settings, but I could feign an interest in him during a single conversation. Harriette can introduce me."

"Delighted," Harriette said in an amused tone that almost certainly meant she was inwardly laughing at one or other of them.

"It is really not necessary," Mr MacPherson quickly said to her. "I have never been challenged to a duel and have already been introduced to the gentleman; I can speak to him without causing the least disagreement."

"Better not to take any chances," Harriette told him, with a welcoming show of support.

Mr MacPherson opened his mouth and Ishbel said quickly, "It is settled then."

Looking thoroughly disgruntled, he said, "Apparently," then added, "Did you attend any lectures today?"

"Eight," she said, a little startled by the abrupt change of subject.

"Is human anatomy one of your interests?"

"Yes. Why?"

"I happen to have observed that the books on the subject show the kind of pictures that are thoroughly unsuitable for an unmarried lady. I trust your professors know better than to let you see such things?"

"In fact," she told him, "the professors know better than to tell me what I can and cannot study."

"It does not appear as if I am needed here, so I will bid you both good evening." He got up, bowed stiffly, ignored Harriette's dismissive gesture with her fan, and stalked out of the room.

Ishbel watched him leave with an anger that swiftly turned into dismay. How had that argument even begun? He had given no reason for his dislike at the thought of her speaking to the Duke of Lothian and the comment about her studying had come from nowhere. Also how had it come about that she had insisted on showing an interest in a man she had never met to get information from him when she had no idea how to charm anyone into doing anything?

She turned to Harriette as the older woman got to her feet and headed to the parlour door, saying, "I am starting to like that young man. He can always be relied upon to enliven a dull evening."

15. A DISAGREEABLE AFTERNOON

ISHBEL AWOKE in an irritable mood, having slept extremely badly. She felt, although she could not have explained why, as if she had Harriette to blame for the disagreement with Mr MacPherson. She had begun to believe he would remain her friend and would not vanish from her life as other people had, but now she was not certain of it. Had his reaction last night meant that he had objected to her studying all along and only feigned interest in it or had she done something to upset him? Perhaps someone else had annoyed him.

She washed, let Lucy tie her into her stays and pulled on a plain gown, then hurried down to the dining room, where Harriette was choosing her breakfast and Lord Huntly was already buried behind his morning newspaper.

"Did you say something to annoy Mr MacPherson before I got home yesterday?" she asked as she picked up a plate.

Harriette added scrambled eggs to her plate. "Why would I possibly do that?"

"That was not a *no*."

"He was in a perfectly amiable mood until your arrival."

Ishbel deflated. "Oh."

"You can meet me here at two o'clock but make sure you are already changed into something smarter and more becoming." Harriette looked at the gown Ishbel currently wore and shuddered. "Perhaps you should just let me choose the fabric and style of your outfits from now on."

"You tried that," Ishbel reminded her, recalling her first year living under the same roof as her cousin. "It did not end well."

"You can be excessively stubborn."

"Would you let anyone else choose your clothes?"

Harriette looked horrified at the idea. "Of course not." She added

71

a roll to her plate and walked over to the dining table, taking a seat opposite her husband. "But I have good taste."

Ishbel threw a frown at the back of her coiffed head then thought to ask a more important question: "Why am I meeting you at two o'clock?"

"To be introduced to the Duke of Lothian obviously. He will be one of my guests for afternoon tea today."

Well, she could hardly object when she did need to meet him and at least it did not interfere with any of her timetabled lectures today. "Do you think I should inform Mr MacPherson?" She hoped he would be in a better mood today and they could ignore their tiff.

As she carried her food to the table and sat down, she caught her cousin looking at her with a disbelieving expression, but Harriette just said, "You should do whatever you wish."

Those were the most un-Harriette-like words ever spoken and Ishbel began to view the upcoming day with trepidation. She attended her morning lectures, including watching the dissection of a cadaver during an anatomy class, which was fascinating and which Mr MacPherson would thoroughly have disapproved of. She had no idea what to do about him. She was tempted to just ignore him, but in the end she decided he was owed an update on the case so she wrote him a short note saying when she would meet the duke and that he was welcome to call at the house later this afternoon should he wish to discuss the outcome.

She then got changed into a brightly coloured robe à la polonaise, its mass of gathered skirts too big and elaborate for her tastes, but it was part of her strategy for handling the duke. She had told Lucy what she was doing and confessed her unease.

As she did up all the tiny buttons at the back of the dress, Lucy now said, "It'll be easy for you, miss. If he has the new horses with him, you can just comment on them, smile at him and let him talk for the rest of the afternoon. Men like being listened to, so he should tell you everything you want to know without you doing a thing."

That sounded reassuringly simple. Ishbel tied a lace fichu over her shoulders and, with a frown, surveyed her image in the mirror, trying to imagine how a man would see her. The sky-blue dress went well with her red hair and was likely to draw attention to her in a way she usually hated, but she could put it to use on this occasion. They needed to know if the duke was the thief.

"You are certain I will not need to say anything in particular, or simper?"

Lucy observed her with fond amusement. "Can you simper, Miss?"

"No."

"Then best not. If he ever shows signs of losing interest in talking to you just compliment him. Tell him he has good taste in horses or clothes or whatever he's talking about. That should set him off again."

"How can you know so much about such matters, Lucy?"

"I watched my oldest sister court her husband," her maid said, folding up the gown Ishbel had worn this morning.

"It was not the other way around?"

"No, miss," Lucy said with a grin. "Meggy wanted John from the moment she first saw him and barely let him out of her sight 'til she got him."

"And they married?"

"Married with four children now and he always says he doesn't know how he managed without her."

With this tale in her mind, Ishbel headed down the curving staircase to the drawing room to meet Harriette, who looked her over and pronounced her appearance acceptable. The afternoon's guests then began arriving, half a dozen in all, including Lady Tinbough whom Ishbel had not known was coming. Not wanting the other guests alerted of her investigation, Ishbel was relieved, although also a little surprised, when Lady Tinbough failed to mention the robbery or ask how close they were to finding the thief. Perhaps Harriette had warned her of the plan for the afternoon.

The Duke of Lothian was one of the last to appear and Ishbel watched with relief from the three-paned sash window as he pulled up in front of the house in a shiny phaeton and the two new white geldings. Harriette introduced Ishbel to him and the usual bow and curtsy were exchanged. He was a handsome man, but Ishbel detected an autocratic look in his bright blue eyes and a sternness in the thick black brows over them.

She smiled up at him with what she hoped looked like admiration and said, "What beautiful horses you have brought with you."

"It does you credit that you noticed their quality," he said in a condescending tone. "They are new and must be two of the fastest thoroughbreds in Edinburgh. Perhaps you would allow me to demonstrate and ride you round the local park?"

That was the last thing she wanted so she said noncommittally, "How kind of you to suggest it," then, before he could set a date for the excursion, asked the first thing that came into her head, "How are you enjoying the Season?"

"I spend half my time in London, which I prefer. I am a member of the Tory party and have been called on considerably for my opinion in connection with recent riots and the worsening situation in France."

He looked at her as if expecting a response so she said, "How interesting," while wondering how she could possibly steer the conversation to the awkward subject of his finances or lack thereof. She found herself wishing Mr MacPherson were here. He had a natural charm that she lacked. Then she recalled that he had not thought she could find out the necessary information from the duke and she determined to prove him wrong. "What activities do you enjoy in Edinburgh?" she asked then cursed herself as an idiot as he would hardly admit to liking the odd bit of burglary.

He did not react to her abrupt changes of subject, saying, "I enjoy the intellectual stimulus of conversing with such intelligent men as Lord Huntly and, equally, take great pleasure in the company of a beautiful woman."

She gritted her teeth at the oft-heard implication that women were purely decorative then, thankfully, before she had to wrack her brains again, Harriette called them over to join the rest of the group, where, upon sitting down, they were presented with cups of tea.

"I hear that you enjoy gambling, Your Grace," Harriette said to the duke. "I fear I have a bad habit of losing money every time I play cards so you must share any tips you have."

"It is funny you should say that as I made a small fortune at faro last week," he said. "You have to look at card games in a logical way that I fear is beyond most women but is not, I am sure, for your ladyship."

"How kind," Harriette said in a silky tone then threw a side glance at Ishbel to underscore the ease of her success at finding out what was needed in the face of Ishbel's failure.

Ishbel glared at her teacup and wished she were anywhere but here where she was doing nothing more than look a fool and entertain Harriette.

Around her, a conversation was begun on the subject of English lace versus French lace. It continued longer than she would have imagined possible then branched off into a discussion of hat styles. Time slowed down until she felt as if she had endured this nightmare for a lifetime.

Of only one thing was she certain: she would get her revenge on Harriette for this.

16. ANOTHER DEAD END

"WHAT DID you learn?" Ewan asked Miss Campbell the afternoon after their disagreement. After sleeping on it and discussing the matter with Rabbie, he had been able to admit to himself that he had reacted out of jealousy, and he felt like a fool. He had been grateful to receive Miss Campbell's note and was determined to behave in a rational manner from now on.

They were sitting in the library – a room she seemed to draw strength from – and she pursed her lips at this question before finally answering, "That I dislike dukes even more heartily than I currently dislike my cousin."

"Ah." He tried to keep to himself his delight that the attractive duke had failed to impress her. "Then it did not go well?"

"I am afraid your assessment of my character was correct. I have no idea how to charm a man into telling me things."

"I promise you I did not intend my reaction to indicate any such opinion," he said, appalled that he had expressed himself so badly and upset her. His opinion was in fact the opposite: he could not imagine how anyone could fail to be charmed by her intelligence, kind nature and beauty. She certainly captivated him. "I simply did not want you to be put in a situation I thought you would dislike."

"*Dislike* is too mild a word for it. I believe *loathe* does not even do my opinion of the afternoon justice."

They both laughed and the tension in the room faded away. She then told him what her cousin had discovered and he said, "Then, if his recently gained money was indeed obtained at cards – which I can check – the duke is not the thief."

"It seems unlikely," she said with a regret that indicated she had formed a reassuringly poor opinion of the man. "Our main suspects are, therefore, the lady's maid who left Lady Tinbough's employ so

76

abruptly and the two tradesmen who called at the house. I do not rule out the other society visitors but, the questioning of them at the ball having caused some offence, perhaps we should not consider them again until we have ruled out the others. Do you agree?"

He nodded. "I do. Since I have not heard anything from the caddie who said he would look for the maid, should we speak to the tradesmen first?"

She glanced over at the table clock. "They will still be in their shops at this hour. If you do not have to prepare for any engagement perhaps we could visit them now."

"I am entirely at your disposal," he told her.

They ran into Lady Huntly on their way out and told her where they were going, Miss Campbell appearing to take great pleasure in her cousin's disgruntled reaction: "Now? It is less than an hour until dinner and you need to change."

"I will endeavour not to be late but, since we are doing this work at your insistence, I am sure you will not mind if I am tardy."

She swept past her cousin, nose in the air, and out of the front door, leaving Lady Huntly to turn her glare upon Ewan. He gave a polite smile and hastened after Miss Campbell, wondering what the current quarrel was between the two women.

Ewan drove them in his curricle, passing a large throng of people close to the city's gallows in the centre of the Old Town, next to the Tolbooth Prison. "Someone is being hanged today," he observed.

Miss Campbell put a gloved hand on his arm, urgency or alarm in the gesture. "Oh, I believe it must be Mr Brodie."

"Do you wish to stop and watch?" He had no stomach for such a sight, but most people viewed it as entertainment, as the crowd here attested.

"No. Were he a killer I would not object, but I feel sorry for Mr Brodie. I will never understand what motivated him to become a thief when he had a good life, but he and his accomplices harmed no one, just embarrassed them. This does not feel like justice."

"I agree," he said, remembering the proud, confident man in the courtroom. He continued driving them to the address of the first tradesmen's shop which turned out, instead, to be a terraced house, as he continued to wonder what motivated someone to become a criminal. For some he knew it was desperation – a man with a starving family would have a reason to steal – and for others a bad temper or too much alcohol might produce a violent outburst. But when someone had everything they could want, as Mr Brodie had seemed to have, what prompted them to fall into such a dangerous life?

He helped Miss Campbell from the curricle, her small gloved hand fitting perfectly inside his. The street clearly housed the poorer members of society, the houses tiny and the roads smelly and uncared for but there were no shops or workshops visible. They knocked on the door as Ewan wondered if an error had been made with the unlikely address, but it was opened by a muscular man several inches taller than Ewan who confirmed himself as Mr Roberts, the chimney sweep.

He led them into the kitchen where a couple of boys were playing at dice and shooed them out.

"The matter is rather delicate," Miss Campbell said, sitting on a stool at the uneven kitchen table in the grimy room as if completely at home there, "and I want to make it clear that we are not accusing anyone of anything, simply searching for information. Lady Tinbough has had a valuable emerald necklace stolen within the last couple of weeks and we were told that Pete, one of the boy's you employ, visited to sweep the chimneys during that time."

Mr Roberts, who stood leaning against a kitchen counter in the tiny room, yelled for the boy in question and one of the lads came back in. The boy was around ten, with an under-fed scrawny look, and must have been working today as his face, arms and clothes were covered in black smudges.

"Pete, have you ever seen any jewellery in Lady Tinbough's house?"

"Aye, Mr Roberts. The rich ladies and gents are always wearing glittery things."

"Did you ever take anything like that?"

The boy's eyes widened and darted to each of them then back to his employer. "No, Mr Roberts – I swear!"

"If you're lying I'll find out." Roberts folded muscular arms and glowered at the boy who flinched and backed away.

"I'm not, I promise," he said, speaking rapidly. "You can search me and search my home. I wouldn't be that dumb, sir. I know what happens to thieves."

"We believe you, Pete," Ewan said, bothered by the boy's distress.

He patted his tiny shoulder but the boy only relaxed when Roberts' expression eased. "Did you ever see anyone else with jewellery – someone that it didn't belong to, like a maid or visitor?"

Pete glanced at Roberts before answering. "No, sir."

"Thank you," Miss Campbell said, smiling at the laddie. "You've been very helpful." She gave him a coin which he pocketed with a thank you, brightening.

"All right. Get!" Roberts said and the boy ran out.

"We appreciate your assistance, Mr Roberts," Ewan said, letting the man show them back through the dim, narrow corridor to the front door.

"People employ me because they know I'm honest and my boys get that. I'd never be involved in any theft and neither would they."

"We understand," Ewan said, "Thank you."

They stepped outside, the brightness a contrast to the interior of the house even though the day was an overcast one. A few small children were playing outside and Ewan watched them, thinking of the boys inside and the drudgery of their lives. He was aware that young boys were always used for such work as they were small enough to fit up the chimneys, but it had always bothered him.

"It is not right to see children having to work," Miss Campbell said, echoing his thoughts.

"No, it is not." A woman walked past them and gave him an interested look, her rouged cheeks and lips and the patches on her face, that might hide signs of disease, suggesting she might be a prostitute. This was no neighbourhood for Miss Campbell to linger in. He put a hand on her arm and they walked back to the curricle. He helped her up then walked round it and got in, taking the reins.

"We can visit the other tradesman tomorrow," he suggested as the horses trotted forward, leading them back to Miss Campbell's home.

"Could we go and see the maid's family first?" she said. "If she is the guilty one then I suspect there is more to all this than we know and the sooner we can locate her the better. Even if she is not the thief it worries me the way she left Lady Tinbough's house and I would like to find out if she needs help."

"Certainly," he agreed. Knowing there was nothing they could do for the working children like the chimney sweep's boys, it would be good to find someone they could assist. That was, as long as the maid was not the thief. If she was, then it was unlikely anyone could do anything for her – her fate would probably be the same grim one William Brodie had faced today.

17. A DISTURBING GIFT

"SIR, YOU need to see this."

Ewan was breakfasting early ready to meet Miss Campbell. Without his usual late-night outings, it was not as difficult to begin the day at this hour as he had imagined just a few weeks ago. It meant he was neglecting his friends, which he regretted, but this was more important and, also, he had not entirely forgiven McDonald for his insulting comments about Miss Campbell. The lack of support from both his friends had been a blow, but he hoped, in time, to show them how wrong they had been about her.

Ewan sat at his large, polished dining table, a medical book open in front of him, and took in Angus's frowning expression and the item he was holding. He got up and walked forward to study the object: the flowers were painted black; it was a funeral wreath. What was his footman doing with a funeral wreath? "I do not understand," he said. "Where did this come from?"

"It was delivered here," Angus said, "left on the doorstep with your name on the card. You haven't had a relation die, have you, sir?"

"No, I have not." It struck Ewan as he looked at this symbol of death that it was a warning, although he could hardly believe such a thing. Their investigation into the robbery must have come to the thief's attention – they must be closer to catching the culprit than they knew and the person had had the effrontery to threaten him with this.

"Might I ask if this is about the missing necklace, sir?" Angus said.

"Yes, I believe it is."

Angus held the wreath further away from him, looking at it with dislike. "What will you do?"

"I will catch the thief and see them punished. Destroy the wreath – burn it."

"Yes, sir and... if there's anything further I can do to assist you in finding such a low rascal, just say."

Ewan smiled, appreciating the show of support against behaviour that had left him angry and rattled. "Thank you."

It was only after Angus had left that another thought occurred to Ewan that turned his blood cold. What if Miss Campbell had also been threatened like this?

He abandoned his half-eaten food and called for his curricle to be brought round, donning hat and gloves before hurrying out. He drove the horses as quickly as the streets would allow to the Huntly residence and jumped down, striding to the door and knocking sharply upon it.

After what felt like an interminable wait, the family butler opened it and Ewan asked him, "Has anyone delivered anything to Miss Campbell today or left anything on the doorstep?" The man frowned, presumably thinking this was none of his business. "Please. I need to know. I am worried something might have been sent as a... cruel joke. I am concerned only that she be spared any unpleasantness."

"Nothing has been delivered or left here for any of the family, sir," the butler told him and Ewan leaned against the door, overcome with relief.

"Are you well, sir? Perhaps you should come inside and have a seat."

"Mr MacPherson?" It was Miss Campbell's voice and he looked behind the butler to see her standing in the hallway, young and innocent. It struck him at that moment that he was in love with her. He had not known the depth of his feelings before now but he could no longer imagine a life without her in it and the thought that she might have been distressed or, worse, harmed was unbearable.

She walked forward, ginger curls dancing, as the butler opened the door wider to admit him. Ewan stepped inside, fixing a smile on his face that felt unnatural in the aftermath of his fear for her and drank in the puzzled warmth in her large, dark eyes as she said, "I had not expected you so early but that is perfect. We can go and see the maid's family and try to make some progress in finding her."

"Yes."

She drew closer to him with a swish of petticoats. "Are you perfectly well? You look pale."

"I could not be better. Shall we go?"

The butler brought her hat, gloves and parasol and she took them, then accepted Ewan's arm. He could feel the warmth of her hand through his coat and shirt as he caught the butler's eyes on him, puzzled and concerned. Ewan shook his head minutely. He made up his mind in that instant not to tell Miss Campbell what had happened. He did not want her to be frightened and he was the only one threatened – perhaps the thief did not even know of her – so he would keep the matter of the wreath to himself for now. It made it all the more urgent that the thief be swiftly caught and he determined to think of nothing else until that result was achieved.

"I have a lecture at eleven o'clock," she was saying as they left the house and she jumped up into the curricle, "but that gives us more than two hours."

She took a piece of parchment from her reticule and read the address off it and they set off, turning off the wide tree-lined streets down side lanes into a grimy street that smelt as if the waste cart had not yet cleaned up the nightly refuse. Ewan could think of nothing but Miss Campbell and the realisation that he truly did love her. He had to prove himself to her before she was likely to consider an offer of marriage.

Should he have told her about the wreath? He changed his mind a dozen times during the short ride before deciding that she could come to no harm as long as she was with him or her family. If Ewan received any more serious threat, then he would tell her everything and beg her to let him handle this alone.

Lost in his thoughts, he barely noticed when they reached their destination. He helped Miss Campbell down from the curricle, once more acutely aware of the shared touch and of having her close to him, close enough to smell the soap she used and catch the faint whiff of ink.

"Why are you smiling?" she asked, hand still in his, as they stood on the pavement in the dingy street. She had her head tipped slightly to one side and wore the trace of a smile in answer to his. Ewan's heart did a strange little dance in his chest.

"I am just glad to be here with you," he said.

"Investigating?" She looked uncertain of how to respond.

"Yes," he lied.

She gave him a quizzical smile then let go of his hand and turned towards the house. She knocked on the door and a woman in a faded dress opened it. She had the kind of face often seen in the poorest people of looking old before her time, worn out eyes in an unlined face and grey in the brown hair. She seemed shocked to find such well-to-do people on her doorstep.

"Could we speak to you about Aileas, Mrs Jones?" Miss Campbell asked gently.

"Er, yes. Please come in," she said, leading them into a narrow room that was the equivalent of a parlour. Two girls of around seven sat on the floor playing with a straw doll and took in the guests with wide eyes. When Ewan and Miss Campbell turned down her offer of tea they all sat down and Mrs Jones asked, "Do you know where Aileas is?"

"We had hoped to ask you that," Miss Campbell said and Mrs Jones slumped slightly in her chair. She had the end of a bruise on her jaw, the colour pale yellow with a hint of purple.

"She hasn't been home in nearly a month," Mrs Jones said with a tremble in her voice. "I don't know what to think. What do you want with her?"

"Only to help," Miss Campbell promised and Ewan watched as Mrs Jones looked hard at her, then the change in the woman's expression when she decided to trust them.

"Were you told that she vanished from her job without giving any notice?" Ewan said.

"Aye. The butler came round, angry about it, but I couldn't tell him anything. If someone upset her or scared her away from Lady Huntly's house, she didn't say anything to me or her Da about it."

"Then why did you think she might have been afraid?" Ewan thought of the wreath and how much easier a young girl would be to scare.

"That's the only reason she would've left. She was so proud when she got that job. We all were. She's only sixteen and to be a lady's maid at that age is a big achievement."

"Did she get along with everyone there?" Miss Campbell asked. "Was there anyone she didn't like or anyone who made things difficult for her?"

"No one that she said, but she isn't one to complain."

"Perhaps she found Lady Tinbough a difficult employer," Miss Campbell suggested. "It has been suggested that Her Ladyship can be a bit bad-tempered with servants."

"Aileas would never run off like that over some harsh words. She was grateful to be there. Even if she wanted to leave she would've put in her notice. Without a character reference she won't ever get another job that good. It would've taken something really bad happening to make her run away like that."

They took their leave of Mrs Jones at this point, promising to let her know when they found Aileas.

"We have to find out what happened to her," Miss Campbell said as he helped her back onto the curricle.

"From what Mrs Jones said of her character I find it hard to believe that Aileas is the thief." Ewan took his place beside her.

"I do not care about that. If she is in trouble then that is far more important than the necklace."

"I agree," Ewan said, "but if she is hiding from something or someone then she could be extremely difficult to find."

"If we can determine why she left her job then that could lead us to her. I will speak to Lady Tinbough's servants again this afternoon."

"I will accompany you."

"That is not necessary," she said. "They might be more forthcoming with a woman, particularly the maids."

"Then I will wait for you outside the house," Ewan said. "Please humour me on this. I am beginning to think there might be some sinister aspects to this entire matter that we do not yet understand and that could make it dangerous." He thought again of the wreath. "Promise me you will not look into any part of this alone. I would never forgive myself if you came to harm."

She nodded. "You have my word. We will solve it and find Aileas together."

18. TAKING RISKS

ISHBEL RAN gloved fingers over an intricately engraved pine coffee table, feeling the swirling leaves and vines carved into the pale wood.

Since they still had more than an hour before she had to be at the College, she and Mr MacPherson had agreed to speak to the carpenter who had visited Lady Tinbough's home. Ishbel cared less about this than finding out about Aileas but, like Mr MacPherson, she felt that the maid had almost certainly not committed the theft and they had made a commitment to solve the crime, so they still needed to find the real culprit. Besides, with no further information on Aileas, unless they heard from the caddie looking for her, Ishbel could think of no way of finding her, not that she intended to give up; far from it.

"This is beautiful work, Mr McDougal," she said. "I am not surprised that you are employed by some of the wealthiest households."

"That's kind of you to say," the carpenter said but the expression in his grey eyes remained hard. He was a slender, well-dressed man with a strong, local accent. "You told me there'd been a theft?"

"Lady Tinbough has had an emerald necklace stolen from her," Mr MacPherson said. "It happened during the last couple of weeks and we wondered if you had seen anything suspicious at the house."

"You mean, you wondered if I took it. I didn't."

"Mr McDougal, we have spoken to a couple of dozen people about this – anyone who works at the house or visited it during that period," Miss Campbell said. "We have no reason to suspect you of the crime. We just need to look into every possibility. I promise that we will do nothing to harm your good reputation as long as you are innocent."

"Thank you, miss," he said in a less hostile tone. "I haven't ever seen an emerald necklace, either being worn by Lady Tinbough or lying about. I normally arrange to make any furniture repairs when the house owners are out, so the noise dinnae annoy them, so I've never spoken to her ladyship. It was Lord Tinbough who saw a dining table and matching chairs I made for another gentleman and hired me the first time. That was several years ago. Why would I risk a good career to suddenly steal something? That Deacon Brodie's made the upper classes think no craftsman can be trusted but we're nae idiots – he got hanged in the end for his thefts, didn't he?"

"Yes, he did," Ishbel said. She had only discovered after the event that Harriette had attended the hanging. After years of attending anatomy classes, Ishbel was not squeamish over death, but found the pleasure others took from watching a hanging macabre.

They left Mr McDougal and, with no evidence against him and no obvious motive, they were satisfied to take him at his word. Mr MacPherson drove her to Edinburgh University so she could attend several lectures, arranging to collect her later to go and speak to Lady Tinbough's servants again. As she walked through the corridors and up the stairs of the College she nodded to familiar faces among the mass of young men who were students here and exchanged greetings with a professor who had been friends with her father. She took a seat towards the middle of the lecture theatre and opened her reticule to take out quill, parchment and ink.

As the other seats began to fill up, men chatting around her, she thought of what Mr McDougal had said. What did cause someone to steal? With a man like Mr Brodie there had clearly been something about the activity he had enjoyed. She had studied him during his trial and read the later accounts about him that had appeared in newspapers. She got the impression he had enjoyed the risks, that his respectable life had not been enough for him. In some ways she could understand that feeling and it struck her that she had two separate lives in much the same way as he had and perhaps for some of the same reasons. She found high society life dull – with its balls, dinner parties and endless discussions about clothes and marriage – and she did something no one else approved of by coming here to study. Her life would have been unbearable without this. She had always had a desire to learn new things and had risked her father's wrath over and over again to disobey him and come to the College. She had endured dozens of punishments rather than give it up. She did not understand the appeal of engaging in criminal activities, but she knew how unsatisfactory a conventional life could be. Was that the reason someone had stolen Lady Tinbough's necklace: not a need for the money they could get from it but the excitement of doing something forbidden? But, as the carpenter had reminded her, Mr Brodie had been hanged; was everyone who failed to live by society's conventions punished for it? In that case, what would be her fate?

Professor Gregory strode into the room and, instantly, the conversations faded away. Ishbel put the unsettling thoughts from her mind and reached for her quill and bottle of ink.

19. THE LOCKET

MR MACPHERSON was already waiting for Ishbel when her lectures finished. She found him standing in front of his curricle, talking to half a dozen students who were admiring the carriage and petting the horses. He was good with people, she thought, watching him smile at something one of the men had said, and did not set himself apart from those who were different from himself, whether students, tradesmen or servants. He was better with the students than she was and she had been in and out of the College her whole life.

He turned his head, caught sight of her and his eyes warmed while his smile broadened. She felt that smile in her entire body, like a touch. Trying to ignore the sensations, but unable to stop herself giving him an answering smile, she walked up to him.

He said goodbye to the students who headed off, some of them giving her polite bows, and Mr MacPherson fixed his full attention on her. "Did you enjoy your lectures?"

"I did," she said. "They were extremely instructive."

"Did I tell you that I had bought some medical texts to learn something of your interests?"

Warmth ran through her at the thought that he should have not just made this effort for her, but also that it meant he accepted this part of who she was, in a way no one else had ever been able to do. "You did not mention it, but I cannot express how happy I am to hear that. How are you getting on with them?"

"They are not subjects I have ever given thought to before, but I think I am beginning to see the appeal of them. Reading such information opens one's mind to how complex the things we take for granted can actually be."

"It makes you see the world as a more extraordinary place," she suggested and he grinned, nodding.

"Exactly!"

She asked him the names of the books as they got into the curricle and suggested a couple of others that were an excellent introduction to the subjects. By the time they arrived at Lady Tinbough's large home, she was so caught up in their conversation that she had almost forgotten why they were here.

"I was thinking that perhaps I could speak to the male servants and you could speak to the female ones. What do you think?"

"Yes, certainly," she agreed. "And our main concern is to ascertain what caused Aileas Jones to leave in the night."

"It is, although we can also check if they have remembered or thought of anything pertaining to the burglary."

"That should cover everything."

They walked up the steps to the front door and knocked upon it. When the butler opened it they asked him if they could speak individually to the servants.

"May I ask if one of my people is under suspicion, sir?" he said to Mr MacPherson.

"That is not the case at all. We just thought they might have remembered something relevant."

"Very well, sir, but they do have a great deal of work to do."

"They are welcome to continue their work as they speak to us and I promise you this will not take long at all," Ishbel said.

He took them below stairs and Ishbel spoke first to Mrs Fraser, the housekeeper in the cramped space of her office. Ishbel had met her during their first talk with the staff, but the housekeeper looked younger than Ishbel had remembered, younger than she would have expected for someone holding such a senior position, perhaps thirty, with dark hair, plain clothes and a friendly smile.

They sat on unadorned wooden chairs and Ishbel asked, "Has anything more occurred to you about the robbery?"

"I'm certain the theft was not committed by anyone here, any of the staff, I mean. I suppose I'm bound to say that, but surely they wouldn't stay here if they'd done such a thing? Wouldn't they have left the city?"

"You are probably right, although there is someone who left: Aileas Jones."

"But that was before the robbery happened. She couldn't have done it."

"It seemed strange that she had left in such an abrupt manner, so we have spoken to her mother, who has not seen her and is extremely worried. Her leaving is unlikely to be connected to the necklace, but I would very much like to find her and make sure she is not in some kind of trouble."

Mrs Fraser nodded, expression serious. "I wish I knew what made her vanish like that. It's been bothering me. She was always utterly reliable."

"She had had the job for some time, I believe?"

"Aye, for about a year. She was a nice girl, but I never felt I knew her very well as she kept a lot to herself. She was particularly quiet right before she left and I remember thinking that she looked as if she wasn't sleeping. Mrs Thomson, the cook, asked her about it, but she said she was fine."

"You have no idea what she might have been upset about?"

"None. I should've brought her in here and got her to talk to me – I wish I had."

"And just returning to the burglary for a last question: who do you think stole the necklace?"

"A visitor, I suppose. Perhaps a tradesman."

Ishbel thanked her and Mrs Fraser took her through to the kitchen to speak to the cook who, along with a kitchen maid, was chopping up vegetables for the evening dinner. A couple of cooking pots were already suspended on chains over the fire and the heat in the room was almost unbearable.

"Have either of you had any more ideas about how the robbery was committed or who might have done it?" Ishbel asked.

The maid just shook her head and muttered, "No, miss," not looking up from her work.

"It must've been a stranger," Mrs Thomson said.

"On a different subject, since her family haven't seen her and are concerned, we are also looking into the disappearance of Aileas Jones. Mrs Fraser said that you asked if something was bothering her right before she left, that she looked as she wasn't sleeping."

"Aye, that's right. I did. She was always a polite, respectful lassie – not all lady's maids are like that, miss; some think they're better than the rest of us. Before she ran off she got quieter and quieter and her face had this strained look about it."

"Do you have any idea what was wrong?"

"No, she never said, but something was on her mind for a couple of months at least."

"Someone gave her a locket," the maid said so quietly that Ishbel could barely hear her.

"When was that?"

"A few months before she went, but she didn't wear it, that's why it was odd. It fell out of her pocket once and she said it was a gift, but she didn't look happy about it."

"You never mentioned any of this," the cook said and the maid shrugged, looking more flushed and uncomfortable than ever, although whether due to shyness or something else, Ishbel couldn't tell.

"So you didn't see the locket?" Ishbel asked the cook.

"No, miss. You don't think it was stolen, do you? She was out of here before the emeralds went missing, so she couldn't have done it."

"I didn't mean that," the maid said. "I just thought it was queer."

"Do you think she might have had some unwanted attention?" Ishbel asked.

The maid just shrugged again and would say nothing more. Ishbel spoke to a couple more people then left, waiting at the curricle for Mr MacPherson, who joined her after another ten minutes or so. They headed back to her home, the cool breeze outside a welcome change after the stifling warmth of the kitchen, and shut themselves in the library to discuss the case.

"What did you learn?" she asked him as she lit a couple of candles to brighten the room then took her usual chair, opposite his.

"Very little, I fear. The men had no fresh ideas about the robbery, at least none they would share with me. They described Aileas Jones as very pretty and good-natured but did not seem to know anything about her life."

"Who said she was pretty?"

"Both the footmen and the under-butler said something of the kind. Why?"

Ishbel said what she had learnt, adding, "What if one of the male servants stole the locket and gave it to her, but she had no interest in him or perhaps suspected he had not got it honestly? If she spurned him they could have had a fight, which caused her to leave so abruptly, and that would make him a very likely suspect for stealing the emerald necklace."

"That is true," he said. "I think you must be right. Then we have only to determine which man it is."

"That will solve the burglary, but not let us help Aileas."

"No, but it would be excellent progress," he said in a tone that made her suspect he had never thought they could solve the crime. "There are four men employed at the house and two more gardeners. Any of them might have taken an interest in an attractive woman but giving her a locket suggests a serious interest. Aileas's young age suggests she would be a better match for the younger men but, then, if we are assuming she had no interest in her pursuer, it could have been any of them. An older man is equally likely to become infatuated."

"If he has now stolen the emerald necklace then he would have a lot of money," Ishbel said.

"You are right. If we look into whether any of the servants have been spending a lot recently that should lead us to him."

She smiled, a heady sense of excitement running through her at the thought of catching the thief.

20. A CORPSE

ISHBEL WAS not thinking about the burglary or Aileas Jones as she walked through the corridors of the College. She was thinking about Mr MacPherson, who had been on her mind more than those other subjects all yesterday evening too. She had been disappointed by the idea that he had not thought they could actually find the thief until now although, to be fair, she had had serious doubts about it herself. She was also concerned about her feelings for him and his for her – she would never marry, so she could not afford to let herself grow attached to him and it was not fair to give him any false expectations. She had told him once that she did not intend to marry, but she thought that his buying the medical books suggested feelings for her that went beyond friendship. She should explain her reasons more clearly. She was not suited to marriage – they would end up miserable, tied to each other for a lifetime with no way out. He could not possibly really love her. She was not the kind of person anyone could love. When this matter was resolved perhaps it would be better to avoid seeing him for a while, much as she hated that thought. He was the first person in her life who she felt had really understood her. Perhaps that was what she should say: that their relationship was incredibly valuable to her, but that she did not want to mislead him into thinking it could ever lead to marriage.

She entered the high octagonal lecture theatre and took a seat, still distracted by her thoughts. She reached into her reticule for her writing implements then noticed that Professor Monro was standing talking to a young man in a blue apron. It looked as if they were arguing.

"Miss Campbell?"

She turned her head towards the voice and saw a smartly dressed student. "Yes," she said.

"Professor Monro needs to speak to you, miss."

"Thank you." She closed her reticule and followed him down the stairs to the front of the theatre, aware of all the eyes upon her. For a moment she was transported back in time and her father had just seen her in his lecture room and called her forward to berate her in front of a class full of people and send her home. The humiliation of that experience was with her as she approached the professor.

"Miss Campbell, this young man says he works for you and that we cannot go ahead with the dissection. Can you explain this?"

She looked blankly at the youth – from his apron he must be a caddie. This realisation gave her an idea of who he was just as he confirmed it: "Miss Campbell, you and Mr MacPherson asked me to help find Miss Aileas Jones."

"Yes," she said.

"That's her." He pointed to the cadaver.

"No, that is impossible." The denial was immediate. Aileas could not be dead. They were supposed to save her.

The boy held something out to her and she took it, not even needing to look at it to know he was right. As she stared in horror at the corpse of Aileas Jones, lying naked on the dissecting table, Ishbel's fingers gripped the small gold locket.

Ewan hurried into the room at the university and looked round for Miss Campbell. A loud sob caught his ear and he followed the noise and saw a woman he recognised. It was Mrs Jones. A man, presumably her husband, stood next to her and they were looking at something on a table that he only slowly realised was the body of a woman, its pallor and rotting state inhuman.

He dragged his eyes from the tableau and finally caught sight of Miss Campbell standing behind them, her face white beneath her copper curls. He crossed over to her as a man in a military uniform left her side. "Are you all right?" he asked her.

She looked up at him with a haunted expression. "Yes, of course. That is Aileas Jones, Mr MacPherson." She gestured to the body. "Someone murdered her."

"Yes," he said, "but I do not understand what the poor girl is doing here. How did she get to the university?"

She led him further away from Aileas's family to say, "Bodies are brought here for studying in anatomy classes. Most are criminals who have been executed but others, particularly those who cannot be identified, also come here."

"How gruesome," he said and saw her wince.

"Such studies are the only way to make medical discoveries and the only way to teach students how to become physicians and surgeons."

"I understand," he said quickly, not wanting to see her distressed any further. "You should leave. This is no place for you."

She stared at him, pale but with a flash of emotion in her eyes he could not identify. "Those poor people have just lost their daughter. No one cares about this case but us. We must find her killer."

21. THE IMPORTANCE OF THE LOCKET

EWAN HANDED Miss Campbell a glass of whisky, watching her as they sat in the drawing room of her home. She looked worn out which was hardly surprising after the morning she had suffered. He had wanted to take her away from the terrible scene at the university right away, but the man dressed in a red uniform had been a member of the town guards and had insisted on hearing how they were involved in the matter, interviewing them both at length, to pass the information on to the local government. When asked if the crown would investigate the murder, the officer had said that there was no evidence that this was anything more than an accidental death and that, the family being too poor to offer a reward, it was unlikely anyone would look into it.

Miss Campbell had been correct that no one else would try to solve the murder but how could they do so? If he had felt ill-equipped in their work so far, this sad development left him at even more of a loss.

"How do you feel?" he asked Miss Campbell.

"I am fine," she said and held something out to him that, when he took it from her cold fingers, turned out to be Aileas's gold locket. "We were wrong about the locket being stolen. It was engraved with her initials."

He looked at the pretty piece of jewellery without taking in what she said. "Miss Campbell, you must let me handle this matter alone from now on. It has become far too dangerous for you to be involved."

Her gaze hardened. "I have been involved in this as long as you and nothing could induce me to give it up now."

"There is a killer involved." He had to make her understand the risk. "Your life could be in danger."

"Then so be it," she said with finality. "I will do whatever is necessary to catch this evil person. I owe it to Aileas and her family. Will you help me?"

He wanted to shake her for being so stubborn or to fall to his knees and beg her to step away from this, but he knew by now that nothing could dissuade her from doing what she believed was necessary. It was up to him to protect her. "Of course."

She gestured once more to the locket. "Someone bought that for Aileas or it would not have her initials on the back."

He turned it over and saw the letters A. J. carved in elaborate curling strokes. "It is possible that someone stole it and then had it engraved," he said, although this sounded a doubtful explanation even to himself so he was not surprised when she disagreed.

"To take a stolen locket to a jewellers would be very risky and why bother? Having the initials put on was an extravagance – the locket was pretty on its own. It is something someone with plenty of money would put on a bought gift."

He thought about this and an idea struck him. "The only man in that household with money is Lord Tinbough. What if he bought her the locket, trying to woo her, then Lady Tinbough found out and fired Aileas, so she stole the emeralds as an act of revenge."

"Then where are the emeralds and who killed her?" Miss Campbell said. "Besides, if she had fired Aileas, Lady Tinbough would have checked into whether Aileas had taken the necklace. It is an obvious deduction and Lady Tinbough is no fool or Harriette would not have befriended her."

"We have to find out who gave her the locket," Ewan said.

"If it was someone outside Lady Tinbough's household then perhaps her parents know. We did not know of the locket when we spoke to Mrs Jones so we never asked about it... But they are in mourning. We cannot disturb them after they have endured so much today."

"She was their daughter," he said. "They will want her killer caught even more than we do. If we give them today to grieve then pay a brief call tomorrow and ask only about the locket and any men who showed an interest in Aileas we would not need to stay more than a few minutes."

"All right. Ewan, she was barely more than a child. What sort of monster could possibly have killed her and why?"

He shook his head, at a loss, part of his mind caught on the fact that she had used his given name for the first time. She would be in danger from now on until they found the killer. He kept returning to that fact, but she knew it and refused to let it stop her, so the case must be solved at once. They had to act, but how?

They were still sitting in silence when the butler announced a visitor for Miss Campbell. A young man was shown in who Miss Campbell introduced to Ewan as a medical student by the name of Mr Brown. He was a sandy-haired young man who looked at Miss Campbell with far too much familiarity for Ewan's liking. He looked to be about the same age as her or close enough to be viewed as a potential rival.

"That was an unexpected turn to the morning," Mr Brown said, taking the seat she offered him.

"Yes," Miss Campbell agreed with feeling.

The young man glanced at Ewan, as if wondering what he was interrupting, then said, "Professor Monro thought you should know what we discovered when we examined the cadaver, Miss Campbell." Before Ewan could object to such things being spoken of to her, the student went on, "The woman had been dead for some time, more than a week, from the state of decomposition. She had been pregnant and it looks as if her death might have been caused by a miscarriage – either natural or induced."

"Induced?" she asked, looking puzzled.

"This is really not an appropriate subject..." Ewan tailed off at her annoyed glance.

At her prompting, the student said, "There are doctors or others who'll abort a pregnancy in an unwed woman although, of course, it's illegal and there's always a chance that the woman will die from the procedure."

"I see. Thank you for letting us know," Miss Campbell said.

The student got up and began to walk away then turned back to ask, "Is it true that you are planning to track down the killer?"

"Yes, it is."

"How exciting!" Ewan rolled his eyes as Mr Brown added, "Let me know if I can help at all, for instance if any more dead bodies turn up."

He left them with this unpleasant thought.

"Was that a friend of yours?" Ewan asked once the student was well and truly gone.

"A fellow medical student," she said, leaving him none the wiser. "She did not wear the locket."

"No," he said, not seeing her point.

"If she was pregnant then the father was presumably the man who gave her the locket, yet she did not wear it and they were not married."

"This is why I wanted you to leave the investigation to me," Ewan said. "You should not have to hear sordid information..."

"I am not a weak child or in any way feeble-minded," she snapped, reminding him unnervingly of Lady Huntly for an instant. "I do not need anyone's protection."

He raised his hands in surrender. "As you wish." The last thing he wanted was for her to look into the matter alone, which he believed she was more than capable of doing if he tried to argue further.

As he took his leave, he wanted to tell her to get some rest, but he feared she would take this as a criticism. He admired her determination to find the killer but was equally afraid for her. This investigation had taken a violent turn and he could not imagine what dangers they might soon face.

22. A GRIEVING FAMILY

"THERE IS no reason for you to be involved in any way with this unpleasant murder business," Harriette said as they sat around the table in the large dining room eating breakfast, the day after the discovery of Aileas's corpse, the air redolent with the smell of hot chocolate and freshly cooked bread.

As Lord Huntly hastily opened a newspaper and raised it as a barrier between himself and the women, Ishbel said, "It was you who insisted Mr MacPherson and I look into a criminal matter..."

"A mistake on my part," Harriette answered. "I thought it would be easy for the two of you to solve the crime and I do not entirely disapprove of your gaunt friend's interest in you."

"Can you possibly be referring to Mr MacPherson?" she queried through gritted teeth.

"He might be unremarkable in his own right, but he comes from an excellent family. Of the very few men to have shown an interest in you, he is the least disagreeable. You should marry him."

Ishbel threw her napkin down on the table and rose, her chair scraping on the floor with a noise that made the footmen wince. "How many times do I have to tell you and everyone else that I do not intend to marry? Ever!"

She turned and marched out of the room, annoyed an instant later for letting Harriette rile her. For once it was not her cousin she was really angry at. Ishbel had begun to believe that Mr MacPherson respected her and liked her intelligence, but he had acted like any other man yesterday, treating her as if her gender made her incapable of rational thought and as if she needed to be protected from any unpleasantness in life. As if she did not already know of sordid behaviour, after spending her entire childhood watching the disaster that was her parents' marriage: the infidelity; the yelling and cutting

101

words; the long periods of silence between them. The idea that she might subject herself to a lifetime of miseries with a man was unthinkable after that.

She recalled Harriette's comments and silently agreed that Mr MacPherson was by far the best of the men who had liked her – the best of any man she could imagine – and even he wished to stop her pursuing this case. He did not see her as his equal, only as a doll that needed to be shut away somewhere safe.

For Aileas's sake, Ishbel had already been determined to solve the murder, but now she had to prove she could do it for herself too, to show that they were all wrong about her.

She went upstairs and found Lucy with a handful of dresses and petticoats. "Is there anything else you want washed, miss?" her maid asked.

"Lucy, I want you to tell one of the grooms to find a caddie for me by the name of Jed Cassell. Ask him to call on me at his earliest convenience."

"Yes, miss." Lucy took the clothes with her as she left.

Within twenty minutes the caddie was entering the library. It was the same man from yesterday who had been told to look for Aileas. He looked slightly younger than Ishbel, maybe seventeen, but had large muscular arms and broad shoulders from years of doing heavy work.

He bowed politely to her.

"Are you still willing to help with this business, now that it is a murder case, Mr Cassell?" she asked.

"Of course, miss," he said without hesitation or any sign that he objected to taking such orders from a woman. He had a lilting Highlands accent. "What do you want me to do?"

"Would you ask around about Aileas Jones. It looks as if she had been pregnant so her killer could have been the man responsible. Just find out anything you can about her recent life and let me know."

"Yes, miss." She held out a coin to him as she had seen Mr MacPherson do yesterday, but he shook his head. "If I find anything I'll accept payment, Miss Campbell."

"Thank you."

He left and Ishbel glanced at the table clock on the mantelpiece. Mr MacPherson would arrive soon so they could call upon Aileas's family. For the first time since his early calls, when she had not been sure how to respond to his interest, she was not looking forward to seeing him. She had thought he viewed them as partners in the investigation, but she had clearly thought he had a higher opinion of her than was the case.

She put some fresh parchment into her reticule and made herself focus on what lay ahead. She still felt bad about intruding upon Mr and Mrs Jones when their grief was so fresh, but Mr MacPherson was right that they must strongly want the killer to be found and brought to justice.

She walked upstairs to fetch her hat, gloves and shawl, donning them before descending just as the butler let Mr MacPherson in. He bowed to her and she curtsied.

"Shall we go?" she said.

"There is nothing I can say to dissuade you from continuing with this?"

She headed past him, a coldness settling over her at the words. "Nothing, but of course if you wish to give it up now that it has become so complicated, then you can."

He caught up with her on the steps outside. "No, of course not."

She ignored his outstretched hand and got onto the curricle unaided, saying, "I spoke to Mr Cassell, the caddie who identified Aileas's corpse, and he is willing to continue searching for information."

He got up beside her in the vehicle. "You should not have spoken to him alone."

"I do not answer to you, sir."

"That is not what I meant. We are hunting for a killer. You do not seem to realise that he could view you as a threat and try to harm you."

"I do see that," she said, "but fear will not keep me from doing everything I can to find justice for Aileas."

"I understand that and I feel the same way. You can rely on my support utterly but, for my peace of mind, will you promise not to take unnecessary risks? That you will not pursue any clues alone?"

Looking into his eyes, she could see only concern, not any wish to dominate or patronise her, and her anger faded. "I give you my word."

He smiled and, as they set off, she began to relax. It was a sunny day and, as they passed the park, she could see people strolling about or stopping to talk to acquaintances. A woman had been murdered, but the world continued on, uncaring. It did not seem right. She could remember feeling the same way after her parents had died and she realised their lavish lifestyle had been a sham, that there was virtually no money left. She had been lost in grief and fear over what her fate would be, while everyone else had continued to attend balls, dinner parties, musical evenings and other entertainments. Even Harriette and her parents had barely seemed touched by the deaths.

They arrived at the home of Mr and Mrs Jones and, once again hesitant over calling at such a time, Ishbel walked with Mr MacPherson to the front door, where he knocked upon it.

Mrs Jones opened it and Ishbel took in the bruise on her cheek. It had been there yesterday, but Ishbel had been too distracted to consider it. There had been a faded bruise on her face when they had first come here too and Ishbel wondered who had caused them.

"Our apologies for intruding on your grief," Mr MacPherson said in a gentle tone, "but we wish to find the person responsible for your daughter's death. If you are up to answering a couple of brief questions it would help us do so."

"We can return tomorrow if it is too difficult for you to face today," Ishbel added.

"No. Mr Jones and me are both grateful to you for what you're doing. Come inside."

They followed her into the sitting room where the rest of her family were assembled: Mr Jones, a boy of around fourteen and the two young girls who had been playing the last time they called here.

"We are so sorry for your loss," Ishbel said to them all.

"Thank you, Miss," Mrs Jones said.

Mr MacPherson repeated the condolences and told Mr Jones why they were here. He then asked about the locket.

Mrs Jones shook her head and looked at Mr Jones who said, "We dinnae know nothing about a locket. I suppose Beathan might've saved up for it, but I don't know why Aileas wouldna have told us about it."

"Who is Beathan?" she asked.

"He's her young man. They've been seeing each other about a year, but I dinnae know if he's serious about her or not," Mr Jones said.

"Could you tell us his address or where he works?" Ishbel asked.

As she wrote down the information Mrs Jones gave, Mr Jones said, "What does this locket have to do with our lassie's death?"

"We are not sure," Mr MacPherson said. "At first we were investigating the theft of an emerald necklace and we wondered if the locket had also been stolen."

"Are you accusing Aileas of being a thief?" Mr Jones approached Mr MacPherson in an aggressive way. He was taller and broader and Ishbel swallowed, not knowing what was about to happen.

"We do not think that," Mr MacPherson said. "The locket had Aileas's initials engraved on it, so it was clearly a gift that had been bought especially for her. We did not know that until we saw it yesterday, but she had never worn the locket, which made us wonder if she disliked her admirer's attention and that was why she left." He showed Mr Jones the locket.

"This is a good necklace – must be worth a fair bit."

Mr Jones looked down at the delicate jewellery resting on his large, calloused hand. "I doubt Beathan could've afforded something like this and, if he thought enough of her to save up for something expensive, why wouldn't he have bought an engagement ring? She's – she was a pretty lass. You think a gent took an interest in her? Maybe wanted her to be his mistress?"

"It is a possibility," Mr MacPherson said. "The locket is, of course, yours now but, if we can find out who bought it, that might be proof in a murder trial of the killer, so it would be best if you did not sell it for the moment."

"You'd better hang on to it 'til you find the man," Mr Jones said, giving the locket back to Mr MacPherson. "There's nothing more important than finding out who killed our Aileas. I'll be asking around about what happened too and God help the bastard if I catch him first."

Mr MacPherson gave Mr Jones his address and told the family he would let them know when there was more information.

Ishbel saw one of the small girls wipe tears off her face before they left and the mother looked red-eyed. Their loss cut at her. Their lives were already so difficult and to have this misery added to the others must be almost unbearable.

She and Mr MacPherson got into his curricle and he said, "Did you see the bruises on Mrs Jones?"

"I did."

"If Mr Jones has that much of a temper how might he have reacted if he learned that Aileas was expecting a child out of wedlock?"

She stared at him, hardly believing she was hearing him suggest such a thing. "What a horrible thing to say about a grieving father! Would you make such an unfounded accusation if he were not working class? I thought better of you than this."

She jumped down from the curricle and headed blindly up the street, ignoring his calls to her, lost as much in her own memory of grief as the thought of the pain in Mr and Mrs Jones's faces.

23. APOLOGIES

EWAN WAS beginning to feel as if he could say nothing lately without causing offence to Miss Campbell and he did not understand why. It stung a little that she had thought he was the kind of person who thought less of working-class people; that was not him at all and he had thought she understood him better after the weeks they had spent in each other's company. They never should have got involved in the entire criminal business – he was useless at this work and appeared badly to her. If he had slowly courted her in the traditional way he would have known how to behave and they might have been engaged by now. And he wanted that. He wanted to kiss her and plan their wedding and future together, not stand by, useless, while she found a murdered girl and wait for something worse to befall her.

He knew he could not talk her out of pursuing the investigation, though, and her refusal to consider her own safety made him love and admire her all the more, as much as it also disturbed him. He felt a sense of wanting justice for Aileas Jones too and it was worrying to think that her death might have never been looked into if they had not been willing to do it. How many other people had to face the murder of loved ones and other crimes and, unless they were rich enough to pay for help, they had to live with knowing the criminals would never be caught? It was wrong, an unacceptable injustice in the way the country treated crime.

He had slept badly after his argument with Miss Campbell and was awake early so, knowing how early her family arose in the mornings, he called to speak to her at eight o'clock.

She came downstairs to greet him, as serious as ever and beautiful enough to take his breath away. "Mr MacPherson, I owe you an apology," she said at once.

"I expressed myself badly," he said. "I did not mean to imply that working-class people acted any differently to the upper classes."

"I was reminded of the death of my parents," she said quickly. "You made a logical comment about the murder, but I was not being rational and I was unfair to you."

"Perhaps we could put it behind us," he suggested, touched by her apology.

"I would be grateful for that." She led him into the drawing room and rang the bell for a footman to get them hot drinks. "We have been looking into this matter from the point of view of the theft of the emeralds. Perhaps we should reconsider what we have learnt, knowing that everything actually began with a murder."

They sat down and he thought this over. "If the locket was not stolen then I do not see how the necklace theft ties in with the murder."

"Perhaps they are not connected," she said, "or only inasmuch as they took place in the same household."

"That would be a strange coincidence."

"We cannot know for certain, but it looks as if Aileas was already dead by the time the necklace was taken."

"Perhaps she saw the thief committing a different robbery or found out he was dishonest and threatened to tell someone and that is why he killed her," he suggested.

"Or, as much as the possibility shocks me, you could have been correct yesterday in suspecting that Aileas's father found out about the pregnancy and killed her in a rage."

"It is possible she was not murdered at all," he said, reluctant to discuss the subject with her but knowing she would want him to.

"What do you mean?"

"Your student friend said she might have died as a result of losing the baby. It is possible that it was a simple miscarriage and that no one hurt her."

"You said that unethical doctors sometimes ended a pregnancy?"

"Not just doctors. She could have even been so afraid of having a baby unwed that she did it to herself."

"Then why did she flee from Lady Tinbough's home?" Miss Campbell said. "I feel certain that that ties in with her death which, once again, suggests murder rather than a natural or accidental death."

"It must be possible to find out if any of the servants have committed a theft before."

"But remember that Lady Tinbough said how careful she was about employing people, that she looked thoroughly into their backgrounds and the butler seemed equally diligent."

He grimaced. "I had forgotten that. Then our main suspect would have to be the father of the child. We should speak to the man whose address her parents gave us."

"Yes. It sounds unlikely that he gave her the locket, but he might have found out someone else did and reacted badly."

"That could have been why she did not wear the locket," Ewan said. "Not because she disliked the person who gave it to her, but because she was already close to someone else, so she had to keep it a secret."

"That is a definite possibility," she agreed. "Then the man her parents said she was being courted by would seem to be someone well worth questioning."

He held out his arm and, when she took it, said, "Let us find out."

24. THE FIANCÉ'S REACTION

BEATHAN MACNEE, the man who had been interested in Aileas, worked as a baler in one of the city's mills so Ishbel and Mr MacPherson asked permission of the owner to speak to him, standing in an elegant office in front of a portly gentleman, known as Laird Stewart to his people, meaning that he was actually as far away from being a lord as the sun is from the earth.

"We have no reason as yet to suspect him of any crime," Mr MacPherson said, "but he might well be able to give us useful information to help us catch the killer."

"And what connection does the young lady have to this business?" Mr Stewart said, indicating Ishbel.

"We are attempting to solve the murder and theft together," Ishbel said.

Mr Stewart looked her up and down in an insulting manner and said, "Then I won't hold my breath on it being solved any time soon."

He gave Mr MacPherson a look as if asking why he was humouring her in such a ridiculous notion, but Mr MacPherson simply thanked him for allowing the interview.

As they left his office Ishbel was in less than the best of moods, but she thought with relief that, in not marrying, she would never have to answer to a man in any way. Why any woman would willingly give a man such control over her, she could not understand.

A boy took them into the mill and pointed out Beathan, who was a strong-looking man of around thirty, a good deal older than Aileas had been. When they introduced themselves and asked to speak to him outside he agreed reluctantly, viewing them with a distrustful expression as he followed them into the cool drizzle outside, just far enough out to avoid being overheard and be away from the worst of the noise and bustle.

"Have you been told about Aileas Jones?" Mr MacPherson asked.

"What is it?" he said, looking from one to the other of them. "What's happened?"

"We regret to have to tell you that she is dead," Ishbel said.

"No." He shook his head, expression dark but with a growing worry in his eyes. "No, that's crazy. I saw her a few weeks ago and she was fine."

"Her body was discovered and her parents identified her yesterday," Mr MacPherson said.

"Discovered where? She worked at one of the fancy houses. She was there."

Mr MacPherson explained what had happened, from when she had vanished from her job to her corpse being taken to the university and Beathan's tanned face grew pale. "Her death might have been an accident but probably not. Medical evidence suggests she had been expecting a child – were you the father?"

One moment he was standing speaking and the next Mr MacPherson was on the ground with a hand over his face. It took Ishbel a moment to realise he had been punched. Mr Macnee turned in her direction and she took a couple of steps away, heart beating overly fast.

"We are not accusing you of anything," she said as a couple of the mill workers ran out and grabbed Mr Macnee.

"Are you all right, miss?" one of them asked.

"I am fine. I was not the one who was struck." She held out a hand to Mr MacPherson and, with a chagrined expression, he took it and let her help him up.

"Do you want us to arrest him and take him to the Tolbooth?" the worker asked, a grey-haired man whom she guessed had some authority over the others.

She turned to Mr MacPherson, leaving the decision to him since he was the one wounded, his cheek red and beginning to swell. "No, Mr Macnee has had an unpleasant shock," Mr MacPherson said, brushing the dirt from his coat. "I do not wish to charge him at all."

The other workers left, one of them glancing back at them all in curiosity, and Mr Macnee offered a quick apology to Mr MacPherson before saying, "You're wrong. Aileas is – was my lass and I loved her. I would never have done that and she wouldn't have let another man touch her. We were saving money to be married."

"Did she say anything about getting unwanted attention from anyone else?" Mr MacPherson asked.

"No. I woulda killed any bastard who tried anything on with her. She cannae have been pregnant."

"We do not have conclusive evidence," Ishbel said, "but it seems probable. Did you give her this locket?"

She indicated Mr MacPherson, who held out the jewellery.

Mr Macnee stared at it, noting the initials on the back with widening eyes and pursed mouth. "So she really was running around with someone else?"

"We do not know that," Ishbel told him. "She never wore the locket nor spoke of another man, which could indicate that she did not want his attention."

"We do not mean to upset you," Mr MacPherson said. "We want to catch her killer and we are still in the dark as to why anyone would harm her."

"How is it two quality folk have anything to do with Aileas?" Mr Macnee said.

"We were asked to look into a different crime by Lady Tinbough – the theft of an emerald necklace – then we learnt Aileas had vanished from her job in the middle of the night, and then she was found dead," Ishbel said. "When we find the guilty person we will send word to you as well as her parents."

"That's good of you." Mr Macnee gestured to Mr MacPherson's cheek. "I really am sorry about punching you. Aileas was special..." He tailed off, broad shoulders slumped.

Mr MacPherson patted his arm and they headed back to the curricle, leaving Mr Macnee to return to his job, another person whose life had been devastated by Aileas's murder.

"Should you see a physician?" Ishbel asked Mr MacPherson who smiled.

"No. I will have some ice put on it later and it will be fine. What was your impression of Mr Macnee?"

"He seemed sincere about not having known she was dead nor having seen the locket." His grief over Aileas had struck her as genuine and there had been no sign of guilt from him.

"There are quite a few jewellers in Edinburgh but the one who engraved the locket might remember who paid for the work."

"Perhaps." Ishbel could not help thinking that there must be a simpler way to find the man. He had paid a great deal of attention to Aileas so surely someone must know who he was.

25. WHAT THE FUTURE MIGHT HOLD

ISHBEL WAS once more dressed in her evening finery, meaning she was buttoned into an enormous dress that hindered her every move and would soon be wobbling about in high heeled shoes. Harriette wanted her to attend the ball and at least Mr MacPherson would be there to talk to, which was her only consolation.

Lucy dressed her hair, pinning it up and teasing it to fullness then decorating it with flowers and feathers and dusting it with white powder so it was appropriately ornate. Finally she said, "Finished, miss."

"Thank you, Lucy." Ishbel stood up and glanced with disinterest in the full-length mirror. The woman looking back was not her or at least not who she wanted to be. She felt like a puppet and was not even sure who was pulling the strings. "You must think such extravagance is ludicrous."

"Not at all, miss. I'd love to get dressed up and have a bunch of men admire me."

Ishbel turned to stare at her in shock, taken aback by this. "Really? Would you not feel self-conscious and uncomfortable?"

"I don't think so, miss. I gather there's fancy food and dancing. I like to dance."

"I never knew that."

"Don't you want Mr MacPherson to see you looking so lovely?"

She quelled an unexpected desire for just that and said, "Of course not. We are friends and colleagues, nothing more. I could never do all the things I wish if I were married."

"Mr MacPherson doesn't seem to mind your studies or you helping with this whole creepy business. He might suit you very well."

Ishbel thought of some of the more bitter arguments between her parents and shuddered. "No, it would just make us both miserable."

She walked downstairs to the hallway and she and Lord Huntly exchanged dejected looks, both preferring an evening with their books to any more outgoing entertainment. His wig and brightly coloured formal clothes made him almost unrecognisable from the sombrely dressed scholar, but the ink stains on both their hands said who they really were. Harriette was not yet ready, so Ishbel wondered if she had time to go over her chemistry notes from this afternoon's lecture. She had not been putting in sufficient time to such work recently and did not wish to fall behind.

"Lady Huntly says the missing emerald business has turned into a murder," Lord Huntly said in his quiet, refined voice and she turned towards him.

"Yes. It is not what we set out to deal with, but we must get justice for the dead girl."

"I see. Be careful, Ishbel. People are not as rational as books – they can behave in an unnerving manner."

"I will," she said, remembering why she liked him. He was so often silent that she almost forgot he was there, his role as head of the household long ago relinquished to Harriette. Despite their utterly different personalities, he and Harriette actually seemed happy in their marriage. Ishbel sincerely hoped that it would never fall apart, although she lacked faith in an institution that tried to weaken and chain women.

Harriette descended the staircase preceded by the fragrance of rose water and the chemical smell from the make-up she insisted on wearing, even though Ishbel had warned her of the dangers of the lead in the face powder. She was dressed in an enormous-skirted blue and gold concoction that made her look more formidable than ever.

"You look lovely, my dear," Lord Huntly told her and she took his arm so they could walk in regal manner to the carriage with its liveried coachmen, Ishbel trailing behind them.

The ball was being held in the public assembly rooms in the New Town and was already half full of richly dressed gentlemen and ladies when they arrived. They were a little late, so the orchestra was already playing and the rooms were overly warm. Harriette was at once surrounded by a group of women, who seemed to accept her commands and insults as a matter of course. Mr MacPherson and the two gentlemen she recognised as his friends immediately came over to bow and exchange greetings before Lord Huntly left to join a group of university professors and the two younger men went off to find dance partners.

"I am somewhat unpopular with Chiverton and McDonald at the moment," Mr MacPherson said, watching them bowing to a group of ladies. "They think I should give up our investigations and return to my old life, spending more time socialising with them."

"What do you think?"

"I think I will feel strange when the case is solved, that it will be odd to go back to spending my days as I used to with visits to friends and my tailor and gambling. It all seems a little frivolous. How will you feel?"

"I had not considered it," she said, doing so now. "I had no idea what I was doing at first and felt a bit of a fool."

"You too?" he exclaimed with a grin, handsome face lighting up. "I felt the greatest of frauds and you had far more ideas about what to do than I did."

She did not recall events in that way at all but was pleased at his response. "I think we have both learned much and you have certainly had ideas that impressed me greatly, such as sending your footman into Lord Tinbough's household and hiring Mr Cassell, the caddie. We would not even know Aileas was dead but for him."

"I have seen more sides of the world than before," he said with a note of chagrin and touched the bruise on his cheek.

She would probably see less of him when the matter was over. "I suppose I will miss it."

"I believe I would like to move forwards rather than back to old interests – marry and have a family."

Ishbel listened to this with a hollow feeling. A wife would almost certainly put a stop to their friendship. "Are you not young for such thoughts?"

He looked startled. "You sound like Chiverton." The orchestra began to play the tune for a new dance. "Will you join me or would you prefer not to dance at the moment?"

"I would rather not," she admitted. Had she been a better dancer she thought she would enjoy doing so with him, sharing the light touches that were permitted at no other time between unmarried people, but as it was she hated the idea of her clumsiness making her look a fool to him. "I do not wish to spoil your pleasure, though.

Perhaps you should ask another lady."

"My aunt insisted on introducing me to a couple of young women and their parents," he admitted, looking uneasy. "It would be polite to dance with them tonight."

He looked uncertain so she gave a smile she did not entirely feel and reassured him. "Certainly it would."

A few minutes later he was stepping out onto the main ballroom floor with a lovely girl who was dressed to perfection and blushed and gazed admiringly at Mr MacPherson in a way that must be flattering. Ishbel would not have known how to behave like that and win over a man even if she wanted to. Which, of course, she did not.

Mr MacPherson had an estate, an important family name and he was an attractive, charming man. He was at home in the setting which she loathed. He had wealthy friends and money of his own. If he made up his mind to marry she had no doubt that any sensible young lady would be delighted to say yes to him.

He would marry and she would go back to devoting herself whole-heartedly to her studies. For the first time, she saw something lonely in her old life, but she could see no way around that: the only way to study and live the life she wanted was to always be alone.

She wrapped her lace shawl more tightly around her against a chill in the air.

26. A POSSIBLE KILLER

"WHICH WAISTCOAT will you wear, sir?" Rabbie held up two options.

"Whichever you like," Ewan said, barely glancing at them, and received a sour look from his valet. His clothes had been in a soiled state after he was punched and landed on the grimy cobbled stones at the mill yesterday, although Rabbie had generously shown more concern over his injured cheek, wrapping ice in linen and insisting Ewan keep it pressed to his face for at least half an hour to reduce the swelling. It still felt tender and a bit sore today but nothing to complain about, certainly nothing to have warranted the fuss Chiverton and McDonald had made last night. Chiverton's reaction had, at least, been worry for Ewan, whereas McDonald seemed only bothered about how such unorthodox behaviour would affect his reputation, which was far less important to Ewan than letting a killer go free. He found it frustrating that his oldest friends made no effort to understand his feelings on the subject. Chiverton, at least, should comprehend the need to be true to oneself given that he had a male lover and refused to marry.

Both men wanted Ewan to drop the murder investigation, saying he was mad to even think of looking into it, let alone dragging Miss Campbell into such a dangerous business. That had stung his conscience, but she understood the dangers and Aileas's death had distressed her, so it was her right to pursue the killer just as much as it was his, which she would certainly do with or without his assistance.

No, his main concern from last night was Miss Campbell's response to the mention of marriage. Had her comment about his age meant that, at eighteen, she considered herself too young to marry him? He had no objection to a long engagement. But she had not looked as if the idea appealed at all. Surely she cared for him? He had let himself believe she shared his feelings, but maybe he was wrong. She had never behaved as other young ladies did, blushing or flirting with him, but he had just thought that such reactions were not in her character. Her face had an impassive quality that gave away little of her feelings.

He finished getting dressed with none of his usual attention and Rabbie said, "This murder business has you worrying about things you should never have had to deal with. The sooner it's over the better you'll feel."

After his friend's comments the previous evening, Ewan had had more than enough of people telling him what he should do and how he should feel, so he just made a non-committal sound in response and headed down to breakfast.

It was early when he arrived at Miss Campbell's house, yet she already had a visitor in the form of the young, muscular caddie they had spoken of last night. Lady Huntly was also in the room, glaring at the young man, but left when Ewan arrived, silently trusting Miss Campbell's well-being to him which was a surprising honour.

"Would you repeat your findings to Mr MacPherson, Mr Cassell?"

The youth nodded politely to her, hat in hand, perched on the edge of a chair, clearly uncomfortable amongst the fine ornaments and furniture of the drawing room.

"A couple of maids left Lord Tinbough's house suddenly," he told Ewan. "They told me he can't be trusted, that he..." He glanced at Miss Campbell awkwardly. "... he took liberties."

"How badly did he behave?" Ewan asked. "Aileas Jones was probably expecting a child, which she lost." He hesitated to speak frankly on such a subject in front of Miss Campbell but knew she would not want to be shielded. "Is it likely that he forced himself on her?"

Jed Brodie half glanced in Miss Campbell's direction again, looking keen to be gone. "Aye, sir. He did that to one of the lassies."

Ewan paid him for his assistance and the young man fled.

"Poor Aileas," Miss Campbell said as he returned to his chair near hers. "That despicable man."

"We cannot accuse him of anything without proof," he said.

"We should have asked Mr Cassell if he would find out if the maid Lord Tinbough abused would be willing to speak at a trial."

"I doubt he would stand trial for rape based on one person's testimony." He did not say it aloud but the testimony of a maid against a lord would never be taken seriously. "He would certainly not be arrested for murder on this."

"Then we must link him to Aileas's death. Do you think he would admit it if confronted?"

"Perhaps, but if he did not then we would be worse off. He might try to destroy any evidence he has in his possession. Besides, as certain as this sounds, we cannot be positive that he did rape her, let alone that he then murdered her."

"If we can prove he gave her the locket we would at least know our supposition was correct, then we could decide how to proceed against him," she suggested, tapping a finger on the edge of her chair.

"I took note of Lord Tinbough's appearance after we began looking into the missing emeralds so I could describe him to jewellers. If I have the locket with me they should be able to say who they sold it to."

"I have several lectures today," Miss Campbell said, biting her lip.

"I recall," he agreed with a smile. "This is something I can easily pursue on my own and I can call on you late this afternoon to let you know what I discover, if that is convenient."

"Yes, of course. Thank you."

He left her, the memory of that melting smile staying in his mind as he returned to his curricle. Surely that was proof that she felt some affection for him?

After a couple of hours of visiting shops throughout the city, Ewan finally located the right one: a successful-looking establishment full of silver, gold and gems displayed in locked cabinets with glass lids.

"Yes, we sold this locket and the buyer had us engrave it," the jeweller said. He was a well-dressed man of around fifty with hair tied back in a queue and pale blue eyes.

"I need to know the gentleman who bought it..." Ewan began.

"Why?" the man asked. "What is this about, sir?"

"I am investigating a murder – the young woman who received this locket as a gift is now dead. The man who bought this might be the killer."

"I see." The jeweller looked down, frowning, at the small locket on the counter between them. "My brother dealt with the commission, taking down the details of the engraving required. He's back in England now – he only stayed with me for a week. I took payment for the locket but... I have hundreds of customers. He was a stranger, not a regular customer – that is all I remember."

"Perhaps if I described a man we suspect to you, it might help?" Ewan said and, when the man agreed, he told him, "He is a middle-aged, tall, thin gentleman with dark hair, usually hidden by a wig. His clothes are fine but old-fashioned and he has a family ring you might have observed: silver, with an engraved letter T on it."

The jeweller grimaced as he thought for several seconds. "No. I remember no one like that. If he wore gloves then..."

"Then the description could match hundreds of people." Ewan thought hard, trying to recall something else memorable about the man and failing. His idea had yielded nothing and he did not know how they could possibly now link Lord Tinbough to the murder.

27. SETTING UP A TRAP

ISHBEL WAS disappointed that the jeweller had not remembered Lord Tinbough but, as they sat in the library, cups of tea and slices of cake on delicate china plates on the table between them, she told Mr MacPherson, "The important thing is that you found the person who sold the locket and, given a few days to consider it, he might remember enough to identify Lord Tinbough. I kept thinking today that someone else must have seen his interest in Aileas. Perhaps we should speak again to the staff."

"They might say something to warn Lord Tinbough that we suspect him," Mr MacPherson said and took a sip of his drink.

"Then what if your valet goes back there?"

"It might seem more credible if he were to go to the tavern popular with the male servants."

"How do you know they visit a tavern?" she asked, raising her cup of tea to her lips.

"Men usually do," he said with a smile. "It is a place men often visit to socialise, particularly working men."

She nodded, absorbing this information. "I see. Would your valet be willing to help again?"

"I expect so. I will speak to him when I get home."

They glanced round as the door was pushed open and Harriette swept into the room, wearing an elegant dress that matched her red hair. She took in Mr MacPherson's presence with a frown, dispelling the relaxed atmosphere that had filled the room a moment before. Ishbel held her breath, hoping she would not say something rude.

"Oh, you are here," Harriette said to him as she picked up her embroidery, standing over them both. "I wish you would tell Isobel she cannot have anything to do with this hunt for a killer."

Ishbel opened her mouth to argue, but Mr MacPherson was ahead of her, saying, "As much as I hate the idea of her being in danger, Miss Campbell is as determined as I to see justice served, which cannot be faulted. You set us on this path, my lady, and you must know that Miss Campbell will make up her own mind what to do and will certainly take no orders from me."

"Then perhaps she should be given a pistol to protect you both."

Mr MacPherson ignored the implied slight and said, "I have no doubt she would be an excellent shot."

"Then the two of you are as ridiculous as each other. What does your aunt think of you putting your life in jeopardy?"

Mr MacPherson hesitated then said, "I did not inform her of the murder. I did not want to worry her."

"How kind," Harriette said dryly. "Deal with the matter. I will not have the killer learning of your investigation and threatening my family. Solve this matter quickly or I will find a way to put a stop to your inept meddling."

He nodded and Harriette left as abruptly as she had come in.

"I am so sorry about my cousin..." Ishbel began but Mr MacPherson shook his head.

"She is worried about you and she is correct that the longer the investigation goes on for, the more likely it is that you could be put in real danger. Lady Huntly or her husband might even be threatened. There is no knowing how Lord Tinbough will react if he feels cornered, so we must try to draw this matter to a swift conclusion."

"Very well," Ishbel agreed, "but we also cannot act rashly and make a mistake that might leave him free to harm more people."

They agreed on this and he took his leave, not simply bowing as he usually did but taking her hand in his and leaning down to kiss it. The feel of his lips upon her skin was indescribable, bringing her entire body to life.

Why had he done it?

She watched with uncertainty as he walked away.

Ishbel found it difficult to concentrate on her private studies that evening, her mind returning again and again to thoughts of Mr MacPherson and the killer. She cared for Mr MacPherson and liked the signs of his fondness for her, but it was not fair to mislead him. She realised belatedly that his comment at the ball about marriage might have been a hint of his intentions towards her, so she must reiterate her determination to never marry. She let herself imagine being his wife and, for a moment, felt only happiness at the idea, then the realities hit her: a wife was expected to devote herself to running a household and bearing children. First he would insist that she stop attending the university and they would argue, but she could not stand against him – a man could beat his wife if he wanted to. She could not imagine Mr MacPherson doing such a thing, but to marry meant giving a man absolute control over her: he would have her money – not that she had much – and he would rule every part of her life. The man was the master. She thought of Lord Huntly and conceded that this was not always the case. There was another more basic fact that she could hardly bear to acknowledge: her own parents had not loved her so how could anyone else?

She slept badly – she felt afterwards as if she had had a nightmare but could remember none of the details, just a sense of panic.

Mr MacPherson arrived not long after she had breakfasted with her cousin and Lord Huntly. They met in the library, the footmen drawing back the curtains to let in the light, and her nerves faded at the sight of his familiar broad grin. She curtsied and he bowed, making no attempt to kiss her hand again, which she told herself was a good thing. He turned down the offer of refreshments and they sat in their usual chairs to talk.

"Rabbie managed to find the tavern that members of Lord Tinbough's staff visit and he spoke to several of them. One valet did confirm that Lord Tinbough has a reputation for improper behaviour towards the female staff, but the others got suspicious over the questions, so he got nothing more from them."

"Then what if we somehow arranged for the jeweller to see Lord Tinbough?" she suggested. "Surely the jeweller cannot fail to recognise him in person?"

"You could be right. It should not be difficult to find out when Lord and Lady Tinbough are due to attend a formal dinner or other function."

"Harriette might know what their plans are as she spends time with Lady Tinbough." Ishbel said this with reluctance, entirely distrustful of Harriette's behaviour by now. However, when Mr

MacPherson agreed, she had no choice but to send a footman to ask if her cousin would join them.

Some ten minutes later Harriette strode in and, after exchanging curtsey for bow with Mr MacPherson, she said in a dangerously silky tone, "You sent for me?"

"Hardly that," Ishbel said, holding back a sigh. "You want us to resolve the case swiftly so we thought you might be able to help us do so by telling us something."

"Go on."

"We need to know where Lord Tinbough is scheduled to be at a particular time. Are Lord and Lady Tinbough due to attend any upcoming social events?"

Harriette mused on this then said, "They avoid spending any time together where possible, but I believe they have both accepted invitations to Mrs Atkins' musical evening tonight."

Ishbel looked at Mr MacPherson who smiled. "That should be perfect," she said.

"Should I be concerned for my friend?" Harriette asked, looking from one to the other of them with a serious expression.

"Yes," Ishbel said, wondering for the first time what the truth that she was married to a murderer would do to Lady Tinbough. "I think you should."

28. A SHOCKING REALISATION

MR MCBRIDE, the jeweller, agreed to their request to try and identify the man who had purchased the locket from him. He also said he would have to consider seriously whether or not to speak at a trial, a wish to help them obtain justice needing to be weighed against the likelihood of antagonising the wealthy people who were his clients and damaging his career. Ewan and Miss Campbell agreed privately that they could worry about a court case later. For now they needed definite evidence that it was Lord Tinbough who had been pursuing Aileas Jones.

That evening Ewan collected Miss Campbell and Mr McBride in his carriage and got his driver to take them to the address of the musical evening, the summer evening light enough for them to get a clear view of everyone while the dim interior of the carriage let them remain unobserved. They watched the arrival of a renowned pianist, who was greeted enthusiastically by the host and hostess and led inside.

"We very much appreciate your assistance with this," Miss Campbell told the jeweller, who looked a bit uncomfortable being in such intimate surroundings with two aristocratic strangers, the inside of the carriage plush but cramped.

"I do not see how you know that the man who purchased the locket killed someone," Mr McBride said, "but I would certainly not want a criminal to get away with such a crime."

The carriages and sedan chairs of the guests began to arrive and Ewan kept watch for Lord Tinbough's family crest. It was strange to him to be sitting here watching people who were dressed in silks and velvets in a rainbow of colours; to recognise acquaintances but be apart from it all. Would he, in the future, be able to attend balls and dinners without wondering what was beneath the smiles and polite comments? Would such a life not be a trifle dull after all this?

"There!" Miss Campbell said, indicating a carriage that was just halting, the driver having trouble controlling the two lively horses pulling it.

"Mr McBride," he said, "would you look at the man who gets out of that carriage and say if that is who bought the locket?"

"Aye, sir."

They all focused on the people alighting then he and Miss Campbell looked at Mr McBride, waiting for his reaction. He watched as Lord Tinbough stepped down onto the pavement, the gold buttons on the man's coat glinting in the fading sunlight, haughty features and family ring clearly visible. Mr McBride remained silent, no recognition in his eyes.

Ewan's heart fell, disappointment running through him. If His Lordship could not be linked to Aileas they could prove nothing. All their efforts were wasted. The information from the staff about Lord Tinbough's lecherous character was no more than gossip.

He put a hand on the carriage door, ready to tell his coachman to return them to their homes but then Mr McBride leaned forward, a sense of urgency in the movement. When Ewan looked across at him, the jeweller's expression was intent. "That's him. The young man."

Young? Ewan followed his gaze, seeing Lord and Lady Tinbough and behind them...

"Their son!" Miss Campbell exclaimed.

"We got it all wrong," Miss Campbell stated in an unhappy tone once they had returned the jeweller to his house and come back to her home. They now sat in the dining room, next to each other at the large mahogany table, untouched cups of coffee in front of them. The long velvet curtains had already been drawn together, although the evening had barely begun to dim, and half a dozen candles had been lit.

"Not entirely. I have no doubt that the son mimicked his father in the mistreatment of the female servants."

"I suppose we do still have the link that we need between them. What is the boy's title?"

"He is the Viscount Inderly. He cannot be more than sixteen." Ewan thought of the destroyed lives the boy was responsible for: Aileas; her parents; Beathan Macnee, the man who had loved her. Another thought struck him: "He cannot have stolen the emeralds, can he?"

"I would not imagine so. I fear we will never get to the bottom of that. Lady Tinbough will never forgive us."

Ewan winced. He had not liked the lady but pitied her now. What they had discovered would ruin her life and, if they had their way, take her son from her. How would a mother react to such news?

"Should we confront the Viscount Inderly with what we know?" Miss Campbell suggested.

He thought about this – it was not an ideal move but he could think of none better. "We have not found enough to prove he harmed Aileas, but I believe we have done all that we can, that there is nothing more to be found against him. I hope we will be able to frighten him sufficiently with what we know to get him to admit to what happened."

She met his gaze with a fierce look in her dark eyes that held him mesmerised. "Then tomorrow we face our killer."

29. CONFRONTATION

AFTER MR MacPherson had left, Ishbel thought more about what lay ahead in accusing the viscount of murder. He might just deny it, but surely they knew enough to arrest him now? They knew he had bought the locket inscribed with Aileas's initials and given it to her. They knew – but could not prove – that he was the father of her child. Had he raped her? It seemed unlikely that she would have lain with him willingly, particularly since she had refused to wear the locket. Had he killed her when he learned she was pregnant or had he paid to have a doctor attempt to kill the growing baby and the surgery had gone wrong?

It seemed as if they still had far more questions than answers, but a physician would never admit to a crime that would destroy his career and, unless someone had witnessed the murder, which seemed unlikely given that it had probably taken place in his home, there was no way for them to prove the viscount's guilt. The staff seemed to have told all they knew and none of them had linked Aileas and the viscount, so there was no help there. The locket was really all they had and what did it actually prove?

When she finally fell asleep it was with the thought that everything they had learned might not be enough, that the viscount might get away with his crime and the thought of having to tell this to Aileas's parents was insupportable.

Over breakfast Harriette asked, "Have you discovered anything more about this maid's death?"

"Yes." Ishbel put down her cup of chocolate, weary and

depressed. "We know who is responsible, but I fear he might not stand trial for it."

"Amongst our class – if I understand you correctly that it is someone upper-class – public disgrace can destroy a person quite thoroughly."

Ishbel thought about this and felt a little better. If the viscount were known as a killer then all the social privileges and entertainments would be denied to him. He would be shunned. If that did turn out to be his only punishment, it was better than nothing and might be of some consolation to Aileas's parents and young man. She felt sorry about Lady Tinbough, though; she was likely to be equally devastated by all this.

Ishbel attended a couple of lectures, since the viscount was unlikely to receive visitors before around two in the afternoon, when morning calls were usually made, but she was inattentive, her mind on what lay ahead. Mr MacPherson joined her at home for luncheon and they discussed what to say to the young man to try to extract a confession. He, like her, seemed a little nervous but also keen to act: their entire partnership had led them to the upcoming confrontation. Against everyone's expectations, even their own initially, they had found a killer.

Mr MacPherson drove them to Lord Tinbough's home where they rang on the door and asked to see the Viscount Inderly. The butler showed them into the neat, grandly furnished drawing room and Ishbel detected a look of curiosity in his impassive gaze, since he of course knew of their dealings with the lady of the house.

A few minutes later the door opened and the viscount came in, all smiles and bows. Ishbel had not seen him properly before and, foolishly, had expected him to look more like a villain. Instead he was a thin, non-descript young man. He put on an air of superiority that was unattractive but, if she had not known what she did about him, Ishbel would have thought that he was doing so to cover up insecurities. He did not have the look of a killer, but who did?

"I believe you are friends of mother," he said.

"We were looking into what happened to an emerald necklace of hers that went missing, but we then started to investigate the death of Aileas Jones," Mr MacPherson said.

"Who?" the viscount asked, standing holding onto the back of a chair, knuckles going white.

"We have evidence of your interest in her, including the purchase of a locket that you gave to her. We know you got her with child then panicked and forced her to try to get rid of the baby, which led to her death."

The viscount was white-faced now. "How dare you! I will not listen to such scandalous lies."

"You do not have to," Ishbel said. "Your family can listen instead and so can every member of wealthy society. A judge and jury might also want to listen to our evidence against you."

"This is insane," he blustered then said to Mr MacPherson, "You are attempting to slander my good name and I take exception. Sir, I challenge you to a duel."

Ishbel breathed in sharply. This was one reaction she had never considered, a way for this evil man to destroy even more lives by killing another innocent person.

After a pause Mr MacPherson said, "I accept."

"No!" Ishbel said urgently, a vision of his death in her mind. "Ewan, we can prove our case against him. There is no reason for you to do this."

He looked at her with doubt in his expressive eyes. They could not prove their accusation.

"I will meet you at dawn tomorrow," the viscount said.

Ishbel shook her head, ready to protest further, but Mr MacPherson was looking at the viscount: "I agree."

30. A DANGEROUS COURSE OF ACTION

"LORD AND Lady Tinbough can put a stop to this," Ishbel said, when they got outside the house. She began to turn round, ready to tell them all she and Mr MacPherson knew, the door not yet closed behind them, but he put a hand on her arm, stopping her with a gentle but firm grip.

"This was always about justice," he said, quiet but determined. "In old tradition, the winner of the duel is proved justified."

"But that is nonsense!" she exclaimed. "The best fighter will win. Have you ever fought a duel before?"

She knew his answer before he spoke, his character far too good-natured for such things. "No, but I have been taught to use a sword and pistol and can do so with a reasonable level of skill. I have as good a chance as him and I think I believe in that idea: that God will be on my side in proving the viscount a killer."

"You would risk your life on a vague hope?" She wanted to shake sense into him, to shout or beg. "What if you are wrong? What if God does not even exist?"

He gave a crooked smile. "Then I will have to trust in luck." It was only when a sob broke from her that Ishbel realised she was crying and Mr MacPherson let go of her arm and lightly stroked it, trying to comfort her even now. They were standing so close that she could have rested her head on his shoulder, had there not been so unbreakable a taboo on it. She wanted that touch, needed it, but, despite every other rule she had ever flouted, she could not lean forward that small distance. "The case would never have gone to trial. This is our only chance of justice."

The idea of justice was something she believed in; it was a large part of what had driven them to the end of this investigation but now she hated the thought. Aileas was dead: this duel would do her and her family no good. Ishbel could not lose Mr MacPherson.

She gripped his arms, feeling the warmth and strength in them, and looked into his eyes: "Ewan, I would rather walk away from this whole business than have you die for it."

"I will endeavour not to die," he promised.

She quarrelled with him until she had used every argument she could think of, standing in the street with well-dressed men and women walking by, but she could not dissuade him from going ahead with the duel.

He took her home, both of them silent during the short ride, then he left to wait for the viscount's Second to come and tell him where the duel would take place and also, as he put it, to get in some practise.

Ishbel went into the library, sat down and stared blankly ahead of her, almost unable to take in what was happening. How was it that everything had fallen apart and Ewan might die in less than a day? He could die, be ripped from her life as if he had never been a part of it, and she could do nothing to prevent it. She went over and over the events of the morning, trying and failing to find another solution so she could tell Ewan he need not risk his life.

She had not moved from the chair when Harriette found her a while later and Ishbel found herself telling her cousin everything they had discovered and what had been the outcome of their confrontation of the Viscount. For once Harriette listened quietly, making no criticism, while Ishbel's words grew more emotional, ending on her own failure to find a different way to prove the Viscount's guilt.

Ishbel had only cried once in front of Harriette. It was after her parents had died and she had felt alone and desolate and sobbed for hours in her cousin's arms, unable to find consolation in the face of such a loss.

She did the same now.

31. THE TRUTH

EWAN AWOKE on the morning of the duel in an oddly good mood. He could not have said why. His duelling skills were middling at best and he had no desire to kill anyone. It was entirely possible that he would soon die but he found he could not accept that.

Rabbie looked close to tears as he helped him don an outfit the valet felt was suitably solemn at an hour that felt like the middle of the night. Chiverton, unwillingly accepting the role of his Second in the duel, arrived as Ewan was consuming a light breakfast and looked equally woebegone.

"What can I say to dissuade you from this folly?" Chiverton asked, an uncharacteristically sombre expression on his handsome face.

"Did you not use up all your arguments yesterday?"

"MacPherson, I am serious. You must not do this. One way or another, it will destroy you."

Ewan squeezed his friend's shoulder before returning to his plate of eggs. "I do not believe that. Are you sure you will not eat?"

Chiverton shuddered and ignored the suggestion. "There must be some way to prove the man's guilt without having to go through with this."

"I think not." Ewan had been racking his brains over the last couple of days to think of some trap or threat to get the truth from the viscount, but could come up with nothing. Neither could Miss Campbell, which convinced him this was the only solution.

He finished his meal and they headed into the hallway where MacCuaig handed him his hat and gloves and said, "It has been an honour to serve you, sir."

"Er, thank you." Was it his imagination or had that sounded extremely final? He glanced across at Chiverton who was glaring at the butler. They walked out into the chill, pre-dawn darkness and he said, "I am really not a bad shot."

"No, but you are always too good-natured and considerate in any kind of sparring. If you must go through with this duel then you need to be willing to take a fatal shot. Can you do that?"

Ewan was not sure. "I will have to."

The viscount had chosen a spot in the countryside just outside the city to keep the encounter private and, by the time Ewan's carriage got there, the sun was rising, brightening the day and filling the sky with pink and gold. Many of the trees around them were losing their summer green and changing to autumnal colours, so the scene was unexpectedly beautiful. Turning, Ewan saw that another carriage was already here and he recognised its crest and strode across the grass to it, Chiverton just behind him.

"You cannot be here for this," he told Ishbel, who sat inside the equipage. She looked at him with a grief-stricken expression, face pale and eyes red-rimmed and he wanted to hold her more than he had ever wanted anything.

"Yes, I can," she said. "If you intend to risk your life then I will be here to support you."

"But it is not..." He broke off at the sound of another carriage arriving and this one bore the crest he had expected.

Miss Campbell put her gloved hand over his. "Be careful and aim here." She used her other hand to touch her dress at chest level. "The heart is not positioned exactly where people assume it to be."

"I will remember," he promised her then they both looked round to watch the viscount descend from his carriage, followed by his Second who held an oblong oak box which, presumably, held the duelling pistols.

Ewan began to feel less easy about what lay ahead, but then he thought of Aileas Jones – all that was left of her being a vulnerable corpse on the one time Ewan had seen her – and any doubts faded. Miss Campbell's hand still rested on his, the gesture meaning more than he could put into words. He took the delicate fingers and bent over them, pressing a kiss onto the cotton glove encasing her hand. This was not the time to say how much he loved her, but he tried to put the feeling into his expression as he looked at her. He let go of her hand and walked over to the viscount.

"Is there no better way for you to solve your problems with each other?" the viscount's Second asked them.

"No," Ewan said. The man – a towering, long-nosed fellow – had said his name when he visited Ewan with the details of the duel yesterday but Ewan tried in vain to recall it now.

"I must defend my good name," Viscount Inderly insisted.

Ewan thought of all the deceit and lies hidden behind the family name and hardened his heart to the disturbing notion of killing another person.

The Second opened the box he held and, as Ewan took one of the two pistols, he noticed that Miss Campbell had got out of her carriage and was watching. He wished she were not here even as he acknowledged that she would likely be hardier than the rest of them to the sight of blood.

The Second directed them to stand back-to-back then said, "You will take twenty paces then turn around, raise your pistols and make your shots."

Everyone fell silent and Ewan could hear nothing but the faint rustle of the breeze against the tree leaves and his own fast heartbeat. He turned his back, ready to move the prescribed distance, but the sound of a whimper made him look about.

"No!" The Viscount lurched away from the small group, complexion a pasty white. He looked very young: barely more than a child. "I cannot."

"The only way you can back out of this is to make a full confession about the death of Aileas Jones," Ewan told him.

The viscount turned, as if preparing to walk or run away, and Ewan knew that if he did leave now then he and Miss Campbell would have failed in their duty to Aileas. Chiverton moved to his side and Miss Campbell walked forward, joining them on the dew-damp grass.

"It was her own fault," the viscount said, turning round so that he faced them again and speaking with a mixture of anger and regret. "I only lay with her once, but she got pregnant. She was going to tell Mother."

"So you killed her," Ewan said.

"No, of course not." The Viscount's shocked expression looked genuine. "I just told her she must get rid of the child, or her family and friends would all turn her away. She accepted what I said...."

"What choice did she have?" Miss Campbell exclaimed, glaring at him. "None of it was of her doing. She did not lie with you willingly, did she?"

He avoided her eyes. "Girls of that class always put on a show of being respectable, but I rewarded her handsomely."

The locket she had never worn, Ewan thought. She had probably been too afraid of the viscount and his family to throw the gift back at him and she could not have sold it without raising questions about where the money had come from, so she had carried it round in a pocket, an unwanted memento of what had been the worst experience of her life. "You forced yourself on her and then made her go to some unqualified butcher..."

"No. He was a doctor," the viscount insisted. "He was not yet qualified to practise medicine, but he knew what to do."

"An impoverished student who would do anything for money," Miss Campbell said in a hollow tone and Ewan remembered that a lot of her acquaintances were medical students. It was probably someone she had studied alongside, maybe even had a friendship with. "Something went wrong."

"She died," the viscount said. "There was blood all down her body. I told Phi... I told the doctor he must get rid of her, but he obviously botched it as the corpse showed up again and the two of you were already hanging about asking everyone questions about Mother's stupid necklace. I thought I might be able to scare you off, but you would not stop. It was a nightmare."

"Scare us?" Miss Campbell asked.

"He sent a funeral wreath to my home," Ewan said. "I checked you had not received anything, but it made me fear for your safety."

"You should have told me," she said.

"I did not want you to be afraid."

The viscount said, "What will you do? I have told you everything – I never harmed the girl..."

"Rape is a crime," Miss Campbell said, a hard look in her eyes. "The attempt to kill the unborn child was a crime. I believe they will hang you."

When the viscount turned and ran towards a tree, Ewan thought he was fleeing and began to go after him. Instead, they heard the sound of vomiting. When the man was finished, Ewan gestured for Chiverton to help him take hold of him. "Viscount Inderly, I am making a citizen's arrest..." He broke off and turned to ask Miss Campbell in consternation, "What must we do with him now?"

32. EXPLAINING MATTERS

THEY WAITED several hours to call on Lady Tinbough to tell her that her son was in Tolbooth prison awaiting trial, but they still got her out of bed and had to wait half an hour while she dressed. There was no sign of Lord Tinbough, for which Ishbel was grateful given what they had discovered about him. She thought of asking Mr MacPherson why he had not told her about receiving the funeral wreath – it troubled her that, even after getting to know her, he thought her too fragile to know something unpleasant. After consideration, though, she remained silent. Today had been a difficult one and she did not want to argue with him; every time she looked at him she was filled with gratitude that he was alive and well.

They were sitting in the drawing room sipping tea from small china cups when Lady Tinbough finally appeared, wearing a yellow gown that seemed incongruent with their grim news and with her greying hair around her shoulders.

"I was told you had something urgent to tell me," she said after the necessary bow and curtsies had been exchanged. She took a seat on the chaise longue and accepted a cup of tea in a regal manner, "or, of course, you would not have chosen to appear at such an indecent hour."

If she thought this was indecent, Ishbel wondered how Her Ladyship would have felt had she known that she had been up for more than five hours now. She had obviously not been aware of the duel and Ishbel could still not recall those first hours of the day, when she had thought Ewan might die, without going cold.

"You will recall," she said, struggling to find a way to tell this mother that her son was in prison, "that several weeks ago my cousin, Harriette, asked us to find out what had become of your emerald necklace..."

"Oh, it turned up last week," Lady Tinbough said, the corners of her lips turning upwards in a half smile. "Did Harriette not tell you? It had been misplaced – I cannot think how it came to be in the pocket of my blue cloak."

Ishbel and Mr MacPherson exchanged a disbelieving look as Her Ladyship talked. It might have been funny – in an exceedingly annoying way – had it not led to the discovery of so much tragedy.

"We got diverted from the missing necklace when we learnt of the disappearance and subsequent death of Aileas Jones," Mr MacPherson said.

"That poor child," Lady Tinbough said and took a sip from her cup. "I was sorry to hear of her death. Did you discover how it happened?"

"Yes, my lady," Mr MacPherson said, "and I fear you must prepare yourself to hear something difficult."

Lady Tinbough looked from one to the other of them and went still. "Go on."

Ishbel took up the story, thinking the news might be slightly easier to take from another woman. "Your son, the Viscount Inderly, took an interest in Aileas. She did not return his feelings, so he forced her to lie with him."

The woman was pale now and put her cup down on its saucer on the table beside her with a slight clatter. "Continue."

"She became pregnant, so your son persuaded her to go to an unqualified doctor to try to destroy the baby and hide what he had done. Aileas died and the viscount and the doctor attempted to hide her body."

"Where is my son now?" Lady Tinbough's voice was barely audible.

"He is in the Tolbooth prison. He challenged Mr MacPherson to a duel this morning but, instead of going ahead with it and lying further, he made a full confession of what he had done. His crimes are sufficiently severe that I believe there will be a trial."

"He will be tried in a public court like a criminal?" Her Ladyship asked sharply, grabbing her fan and opening then closing it.

Ishbel did not point out that this was what he was. "Yes, my lady."

Lady Tinbough rang the bell beside her. "My husband must be informed. He will know how to speak to lawyers and such people."

Ishbel bit her lip – she and Mr MacPherson had argued over whether to reveal this – then added, "There is one more thing and, if you can bear to hear no more, it can keep and Harriette can tell you when you are ready."

"Tell me," Lady Tinbough insisted.

Ishbel struggled to find tactful words. "It looks as if your son learnt to treat the staff in this way from his father."

Lady Tinbough looked unseeingly down at the fan in her hand. There would be an imprint of it on her flesh from the grip she had on it.

Ishbel leaned towards her. "We are so sorry to have to bring you such information." When there was no response she added, "Do you wish me to send Harriette to you?"

Her ladyship gave the faintest nod of her head. "If you would."

33. SORROW AND DISAPPOINTMENT

MRS JONES had wept to hear what had been done to her daughter, Aileas, but had thanked Ishbel and Mr MacPherson for finding out the truth and arresting the man responsible. She had fresh bruises and, by the time they left, a bleakness in her eyes, but at least she still had three more children to take her mind off her loss and to love her.

"Do you think Lady Tinbough will ever recover from this?" Ishbel asked Mr MacPherson when they were back in the library at her home, Harriette awakened and despatched to help her friend in whatever way she could. Ishbel sat and took in all the shelves of books, hearing the faint sound of birdsong outside, and she had never been more grateful for the refuge she had always found in this beloved room. She had begun to regain her strength in here after the death of her parents, when everything in her life had altered.

Mr MacPherson rubbed his face as he sat opposite her with legs stretched out. He looked worn out, like her the fatigue more than just the early beginning to the day, but he was here, safe, beside her, the danger over, which was all she needed right now. "I fear society will consider this business a wonderful scandal and will make Lady Tinbough's life a hundred times more difficult, but at least your cousin seems determined to support her through it."

"Harriette is a solace in difficult times," Ishbel said, remembering how this relation she had barely known had helped her deal with her own grief and find ways to carry on living. When Harriette was complaining and criticizing, it was sometimes hard to remember that she had a caring heart. "I thought I would feel some satisfaction at ensuring Aileas's death did not go unpunished, but the truth is bringing about so much misery."

"I think, in time, life will be easier to bear for Aileas's family because of what we did. We did not cause all this grief – the viscount did that. I would like to believe that we did what needed to be done... even if the dratted necklace was never actually stolen."

He surprised a laugh out of her at this. "I suppose our days of investigating crimes, real or imagined, are over now."

"Yes."

"It is probably for the best." The thought left her feeling rather hollow and, with difficulty at expressing herself, she said, "I hope, now that we will no longer be working together, that you will not vanish from my life."

"Never," he said, sounding shocked at the idea, which reassured her that she could still count on him to be her friend. "Miss Campbell, you must be aware of the great affection I have formed towards you." In a fluid move, he got on one knee before her. "Nothing could make me happier than if you would agree to be my wife and share the rest of my days."

It was the moment she had tried to prevent; the moment she had dreaded. Looking down at the hope written across his face, Ishbel could not bear to hurt him. Would marriage to Ewan be so bad? She cared deeply for him and did not believe he would ever become a tyrant, denying her the studying that made her happy. But their relationship would change. Marriage would cage them both and any fond feelings they had for each other now would not survive its shackles. How could she explain any of this to him? "Ewan, I once said that I never intended to marry and I meant it. If I could do it, I would marry you, as I know that no one will ever be dearer to me, but it is not something I can contemplate. Marriage would destroy me."

She watched as the hope faded from his eyes and felt sick. He got to his feet and looked about him in a lost manner. "I see. I should take my leave of you."

As he walked away she wanted to call him back but no longer had any power to do so. He wanted something she could not give him. Her fears had proven founded after all: she had lost him.

34. A NEW BEGINNING

EWAN WALKED into the hall of his house and looked about him. He had never before noticed how large and empty it was, all this space just for him and filled with expensive, meaningless possessions.

MacCuaig took his hat and gloves, weathered face hinting at an emotion. "May I express my relief on behalf of all the staff at your continued good health, sir."

Ewan looked uncomprehendingly at him, then he recalled the duel and nearly laughed. It seemed so long ago, but it was just a few hours. He could have died. It had seemed such a pivotal moment in his life at the time, yet now he had barely remembered it. It was good to know he would not have been entirely un-mourned and he felt a surge of warmth for the people who devoted their time to looking after him. "Thank you. I appreciate that."

"There is a young man waiting to see you in the drawing room, sir. I did inform him that you were not at home and might not be free to speak to him when you returned but, nevertheless, he insisted on waiting." MacCuaig's tone left no doubt about his opinion of the unwanted guest. "He is, I am led to understand, an acquaintance of Mr Chiverton and some form of entertainer."

Curiosity piqued and feeling that anything would be better than being left alone to dwell on Miss Campbell's rejection, Ewan said, "Then I will go and find out what he wants."

He strode along the hall and into the room where a man jumped to his feet and gave him a deep bow. He was a striking fellow with brown wavy hair and prominent cheekbones and wore a decently made outfit: navy coat and breeches, blue and cream waistcoat and black boots over his stockings. He regarded Ewan with a nervous expression

"Please excuse the intrusion, Mr MacPherson. My name is Joseph Fillinister. I'm an actor and I work with Alex."

Ewan nodded, recognising the name of Chiverton's clandestine lover. He gestured for the man to sit down again and took a chair the other side of the coffee table. "What can I do for you, Mr Fillinister?"

"Alex said you'd become involved in looking into crimes. I need you to solve a murder."

Well, at least it was not theft – their success at solving those was not good. However, he and Miss Campbell had given up such work; every part of their relationship was over. Still, the man had come here especially to speak to him so Ewan should hear him out and, also, he really needed a distraction right now. "Who is it that has been killed? A relation?"

"No, sir. I barely knew him: Duke Raden was his name."

"Then what interest have you in seeing his death solved?"

"A friend of mine, an actress by the name of Kenina McNeil, has been accused of the murder. She's gone on the run and, if she's caught, they'll hang her. She's not guilty, Mr MacPherson. I swear it to you."

The matter sounded interesting and it struck him, hope for the future rising in him once more, that if he could get Miss Campbell curious about it, the case could be exactly what he needed. It would give him an opportunity to find out her worries about marriage and allay them. She had already said that, were she to marry, she would choose him. He loved her as he could love no one else and he believed she was starting to love him. She had not turned him down out of any dislike for him; there was something deeper troubling her. If they worked together on this case it would give him another chance to convince her that he could make her happy.

"I will need to speak to my friend Miss Campbell about this, since we work together, but I believe we might be able to look into the murder for you..."

HISTORICAL NOTES

William Brodie, who is on trial at the start of this novel, was not only a real man but also someone on whom Robert Louis Stevenson based his novel of Jekyll and Hyde. Brodie worked as a respected Deacon of wrights and cabinetmaker and came from a conventional, fairly wealthy background but he also gambled excessively and kept two mistresses and their children. He was like two different people. Some of the legal dialogue in the first chapter was taken from the transcripts from Brodie's trial.

Other real-life people also appear in this story: the lawyers and judges from Brodie's trial and the professors Ishbel studies under at Edinburgh University.

The main characters are all fictional but the problems they face, in trying to get justice at a time with no police force, are genuine.

THANKS FOR READING

Thank you so much for taking an interest in my books. If you enjoyed this novel please would you consider leaving a review at Amazon or Goodreads as this is a massive help to independent authors in getting our books known. It also helps other readers learn more about the books, so they can decide whether to buy them.

JOIN THE FUN

By joining my newsletter you can get a free novella, "**Harriette**", which tells of the events which turn a naive young woman into the fierce Lady Huntly from the *Campbell & MacPherson* novels. You will also receive a free sequel to "**Complications**", a guide to the historical world and characters from the *Campbell & MacPherson* series and the latest information about my new novels and special offers. Join my e-mail newsletter at my website: https://clarejayne.com

Other Novels Available at Amazon

"The Dead Duke (Campbell & MacPherson 2)" - When Ishbel and Ewan take on the case of a duke supposedly murdered by his actress mistress, Lady Huntly threatens to disown Ishbel while Edinburgh's upper classes are appalled, and that is before the duo even begin looking into the reasons why the wealthiest members of society might have wanted the duke dead.

As they continue to uncover secrets others want to remain hidden, their own relationship is threatened by the public discovery of a scandal from Ishbel's past. Is her repeated refusal to follow society's conventions about to ruin her life as well as her partnership with Ewan, and will they ever manage to solve the mystery of who murdered the duke?

"A Dangerous Past (Campbell & MacPherson 3)" – When Ishbel agrees to help her lady's maid, Lucy, find out why a friend of hers was killed, Ishbel must find a way to end the estrangement between herself and Ewan so they can work together again. Their relationship quickly improves until the arrival of Ewan's sister, who is determined he should end his investigations into crimes as well as his association with Ishbel.

"The Convenient Murder (Campbell & MacPherson 4)" - The unconventional Georgian-era detectives, Ishbel and Ewan, have a new murder to investigate when Lord Strand is poisoned at a house where their friends, Miss Chiverton and McDonald, are staying.

Miss Chiverton seems determined that the murder be solved, so why is she hiding important information about it? Lord Strand's relatives all appear more relieved than grief-stricken over the death and everyone who ever met the man seems to have hated him, so the list of suspects is endless.

In the meantime, Miss Chiverton's father is determined that she should make a decision about who to marry or he will choose for her. The man who is desperately in love with her is the last person she wants and all she can focus on is helping to solve the murder.

As events grow more hazardous, lives change and not everyone will emerge unscathed.

"Mr Guthrie's Double (Campbell & MacPherson 5)" - A killer is about to strike but which Mr Guthrie is he after?

Ishbel and Ewan, are given a bizarre new case when they have to hunt down an imposter who has been falsely claiming to be Mr Guthrie.

The real Mr Guthrie is a likeable man from a wealthy family who wins the affection of Miss Chiverton. This complicates everyone's lives as Ewan's friend, Mr McDonald, also loves her and her family only approves of Mr McDonald as a suitor, so Miss Chiverton will face a difficult decision about her future.

The case soon grows more strange and more deadly when a corpse is found, but it won't be the last death as Ishbel and Ewan desperately work to uncover the reason for the impersonator's deception.

"A Virtuous Man (Campbell & MacPherson 6)" - Why would a seemingly honourable university student vanish one night and never return home?

After Ishbel and Ewan leave Edinburgh, the newly married Mr and Mrs McDonald inherit their missing person case, much to Padraig's annoyance. He is sure the young man must have gone off alone to have fun and Padraig would rather concentrate on life with his new bride than deal with it. The missing man is a devout Catholic, though, so it seems increasingly unlikely that he ran off in this way. They then discover that a second man went missing on the same night as the first.

As the missing person case grows more baffling, it causes arguments between Fiona and Padraig - whose marriage might not be as stable as they thought - and the longer the matter remains unsolved, the more likely it is that the boy will die before they can find him.

"An Impossible Crime (Campbell & MacPherson 7)" - Things are not going well for Ishbel and Ewan. Ishbel is miserable living in the countryside, Ewan hates how much time she spends with the local physician and they have a new murder to solve.

Ishbel was looking forward to returning to Edinburgh soon, but now that plan has had to be changed. She is bored and frustrated living on the country estate where Ewan grew up, while he has plenty to do and spends little time at home. She only has two real friends nearby – James Fraser, a physician, and Emma Lee, a spinster.

It is James who tells them of Lady Ashton's death and of his professional belief that she was smothered with a pillow. Both Lady Ashton's husband and cousin had reasons to kill her, but unfortunately it seems impossible for them to have done so.

James takes an interest in their hunt for the killer, Ewan growing less civil every time he finds him at the house, and then Emma falls under suspicion for the crime. Tensions rise between Ishbel and Ewan to the point where their marriage is threatened and a final twist might have even more devastating consequences for them.

"The Prankster (Campbell & MacPherson 8)" - When is a joke not a joke?

Miss Emma Lee, neighbour to Ishbel and Ewan, is being disturbed by a series of bizarre pranks involving her late father's hat. Unnerved by it and bemused as to why she is the unknown culprit's target, she turns to the duo for help.

They are still living on their country estate, Ishbel having given birth to Meg, their second child, recently. Emma is one of Ishbel's closest friends and she and Ewan believe this will be a quick, safe mystery to solve, bringing no danger to their family. They are wrong on both accounts.

When the prankster's tricks turn deadly, no one is safe. The amateur detectives must use all their skills to protect their neighbours and their own lives whilst solving the riddle of who is responsible and why.

"Murder on Bealtaine Eve (Dumnonia Mysteries 1)" With blood spilt during a sacred ceremony, will the gods forgive her people?

In fifth century Dark Ages England, Morvoren is the priestess of Dumnonia, serving the goddess who protects them. She is confident of her place as one of the most important people in the tribe, with the respect of the king and love of her people. At least, that's what she thinks.

The inexplicable murder of a Saxon guest throws all her assumptions about her life into confusion and makes her fear retribution from her goddess. Forced to work with Uxio, a young

Christian deacon who hates her religion, she must solve the crime or lose her home and her freedom.

Uxio is ordered to work with Morvoren by his bishop, but this tribe brings back far too many memories of a past he has tried to forget. Morvoren's uncanny ability to see more than he wants to reveal puts them at odds and a second murder adds to the tension between them. With the possibility of war between the Dumnonii and the Saxons looming over them, they struggle to hunt down an elusive killer.

This unique historical mystery series is set against the backdrop of Celtic beliefs and one tribe's struggle to survive in the changing land of Britannia.

"Fatal Voyage (Dumnonia Mysteries 2)" - Will Morvoren and Uxio discover a killer or a vengeful ghost?

With the approach of the Samhain festival to honour the dead, the captain of a merchant ship tells Morvoren an eerie tale of a voyage plagued by misfortune, illness and death, wanting her, as Dumnonia's priestess, to help rid him of its source. The captain is sure that the two deaths are from natural causes, since no one could have got to the second man, whose body was found blocking the door to his cabin. Despite this, the Christian deacon, Uxio believes the problems are the result of a murderer onboard.

Circumstances and their different personalities cause Uxio and Morvoren to quarrel yet again over how to find out the truth, so they make a wager to investigate the mystery separately. Each one will try to be the first to discover how two people on the ship died.

There seems to be no link between the dead men and no way for them to have been murdered, but both had their enemies. As Morvoren and Uxio struggle to make sense of the mystery, what fresh troubles will they face? They are both determined to best the other, but will a killer outwit them both?

This is the second novel in this exciting historical mystery series set in the Celtic Dumnonii tribe in England in the Dark Ages, a time of turmoil with conflicting beliefs and cultures.

"The Vanishing Thief (Dumnonia Mysteries 3)" - How could someone disappear from a castle on a cliff with stolen treasure, never being seen by the guards at its only entrance?

The latest mystery infuriates the king, confuses the warriors protecting the castle and needs to be solved by Morvoren and Uxio. While Morvoren deals with a problem with her closest friend and Uxio struggles to cope with a servant with a crush on him, they must somehow work out how the impossible theft was committed.

The subsequent appearance of a dead body doesn't help in the least.

"Murder By Another Name (Dumnonia Mysteries 4)" - When is a crime not a crime? Morvoren, the priestess of the Dumnonii in Dark Age Britain, has to travel most of the length to solve a new mystery that the chieftan, Comux, can't deal with. Kenosaglas has killed his life-long friend, Eudaf, claiming that Eudaf was a spy for the nearby Saxons. If Kenosaglas is telling the truth then he cannot be punished for his actions. If he killed Eudaf for another reason, Kenosaglas is a murderer who will probably face execution.

Morvoren faces a seemingly unsolvable puzzle since no one witnessed Eudaf's death except for his killer. Even the two men's families can tell her nothing helpful and Kenosaglas's own children insist that Eudaf was not a traitor. Her search for the truth leads her to another confrontation with the Saxon leader who once wanted to marry her.

In the meantime, the Christian deacon Uxio has been left behind at Bran Castle and has a reunion that leaves his future in question.

The danger increases for Morvoren, who is under the protection of Comux, the son of the queen who hates her. When her life depends on it, will she be able to trust him?

Read the fourth historical mystery novel in this exciting series set in a time where an argument can end in a sword fight and people believe in giants and pixies.

"Ladies Dancing" - Three people find romance over a magical winter season.

In Regency England Kate and Louisa arrive in London - accompanied by Kate's brother, Will - to make their debuts into London society and find themselves husbands. Kate encounters Mr Templeton, who is the opposite of everything she thinks she wants in a man. He might soon change her mind, though, if her blunt manners do not ruin everything.

Her cousin, Louisa, wants to get a wealthy husband as quickly as possible for her own secret reasons. Why she should soon decide to turn down a good-natured earl is a mystery and Kate is determined to find out what she is hiding. The truth might prove to be more than she can cope with.

There is also her brother, Will, to worry about. As a wealthy, attractive gentleman, he could easily find himself a wife... if only he did not loathe every person he encounters, with the notable exception of the charming Mr Fenton. To make the best of the situation, Kate intends to throw the two men at each other as much as possible to keep Will from scaring off their potential suitors. She never imagines the attachment that might form between Will and Mr Fenton.

Just as the duo are making progress in their romantic adventures, a scandal is revealed that threatens to devastate their lives.

If you enjoy the romance, family drama and humour of a Georgette Heyer story, you will love this festive historical novel.

"**Complications**" - This is a light-hearted Georgian era romance where, in the hunt for the right gentleman, nothing works out as intended.

Amelia Daventry dreams of having the lovely clothes and luxuries her family cannot afford. She intends to use her Edinburgh season to get herself the wealthiest and most powerful husband she can find. The one thing of which she is certain is that Mr Brightford, with his constant frowns and criticisms, is a man she would never consider.

Amelia's best friend, Lottie Harrington, has found the man she wants to marry and just wishes to live quietly and make him happy. Her hopes are about to be destroyed, causing pain and chaos to herself and everyone around her.

Lottie's headstrong brother, Benjamin Harrington, has romantic feelings for other men but his parents still expect him to marry. When he meets a man he can love he faces difficult choices but does the gentleman even return his affection?

From suffering heartbreak and tragedy to fighting a duel, the lives of these three friends are about to become extremely complicated...

"An Impetuous Romance" - Will Adam bring Eloise happiness or break her heart?

Miss Eloise Preston is thrilled when the kind, handsome Lord Adam Delworth arrives in Somerset and shows an interest in her, unaware that his offer of marriage has just been turned down by someone he believes to have been the love of his life. To get her out of a dangerous situation, he asks her to marry him and, believing that he loves her, she gladly agrees.

They go to London accompanied by her sisters, Maddie and Helena. Adam immediately encounters his first love again and he is torn between the two women. In the meantime, London society - with its own rules of conduct - is causing the sisters to make one blunder after another. To add to their problems, Helena Preston is thrown into the company of the man she rejected, whom her father is determined she should still marry.

The lives and loves of Eloise, Adam, Helena and Maddie are all connected in this heart-warming Regency romance. If you enjoy the humour, twists and turns, and gentle romance of a Georgette Heyer novel, this is the perfect book for you.

ABOUT THE AUTHOR

Clare Jayne began writing novels nearly three decades ago, when she was a teenager. She has worked in a variety of jobs, including legal secretary and sales advisor, while continuing to write and trying and failing to get a traditional publisher for her work. She then had a short play performed by the local amateur dramatics group and recorded on local radio, and she came joint first place in a writing competition. This encouraged her to take a leap of faith and self-publish and she is thrilled to finally be able to share her novels with actual real people.

Inspired by such writers as Jane Austen, Josephine Tey and Georgette Heyer, she writes historical romances and historical mysteries, although the mysteries also have a strong dash of romance.

You can find out more about Clare Jayne at her website clarejayne.com.

Printed in Great Britain
by Amazon

62132813R00092